Unspoken Magic

EMILY LLOYD-JONES

Unspoken Magic

 GREENWILLOW BOOKS
An Imprint of HarperCollins *Publishers*

The text of this book is set in Carre Noir Pro.
Book design by Sylvie Le Floc'h.

Library of Congress Cataloging-in-Publication Data is available.
ISBN 978-0-06-305803-3 (hardcover)
ISBN 978-0-06-305806-4 (ebook)
23 24 25 26 27 LBC 5 4 3 2 1
First Edition
Greenwillow Books

*To s. e., for being one of Aldermere's founders
and a dear friend*

Unspoken Magic

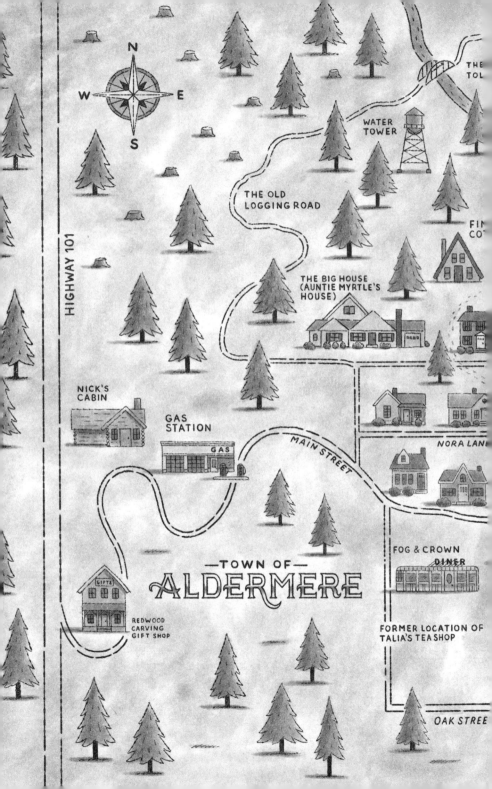

ONE
A Tale of Two Vans

The day the film crew arrived, Finley Barnes was trying to teach a raven to play fetch.

Late-afternoon sunlight slanted through the redwood trees, casting long shadows through the forest. Fin stood at the edge of the woods in her aunt's backyard, holding a ramekin of sliced hard-boiled egg. The raven perched on the garage roof and peered down at Fin with keen dark eyes.

"Coin," Fin said. The quarter flashed between her thumb and forefinger. Ravens liked shiny things, so surely this was a decent lure. She tossed the quarter into the grass. The lawn was overgrown, studded with dandelions and gopher holes.

Aunt Myrtle had been making noises about cutting it, but no one was eager to brave the cobwebs surrounding the old push mower.

Fin pointed at the coin, which gleamed silver in the grass. "Fetch."

Six months ago, Fin had helped Morrigan the raven after an injury, and ever since, the raven had regarded her as a friend. Morri would visit, and Fin would offer a small snack or neck scratches. In thanks, Morri left small trinkets on Fin's windowsill. Fin's growing collection consisted of a piece of blue sea glass, two paper clips, a silver unicorn charm, four metal beads, and someone's spare house key.

"Fetch," said Fin, a little pleadingly. Morri had done this a few times, but never on command.

Morri cocked her head, gaze darting between the hard-boiled egg and the spot where the coin had landed. She spread her wings, and Fin's breath caught in anticipation. Morri leaped into the air . . . and then she made a dive for the bowl of egg in Fin's hand.

Fin let out a yelp and ducked, the ramekin tumbling from her fingers. She wasn't afraid of Morri, but a raven's sudden descent would startle anyone. Tiny speckles of yolk and chunks of white scattered amid the grass.

The raven fell upon the food as if she hadn't eaten for weeks.

Fin rose from her crouch, scowling at the bird. "You're supposed to work for that."

Eddie Elloway burst into laughter. He was perched atop the hood of Aunt Myrtle's old Ford Fiesta, his legs crisscrossed beneath him. He'd been half-heartedly prodding at his math homework.

"She did fetch," Eddie said, in between gasps of laughter. "She fetched all the egg."

"Yeah, yeah," said Fin. But she smiled. It was impossible to feel mad on the Friday before spring break. The trees overhead rustled with a breeze, and the spicy smell of redwood needles was pleasant on the air. The afternoon was warm enough that Fin had rolled up her sleeves, enjoying the sunlight on her forearms. "Why don't you try? You're better with animals than anyone I know."

"I only use my powers for good," said Eddie, flashing her a grin. "And sorry, but teaching your raven to find you spare change isn't on the list."

Fin knew it was supposed to be a joke, but sometimes she wasn't all that sure her cousin didn't have some power over animals. He'd always been good with them, rescuing snails from sidewalks and catching lizards for their science fair project. He always knew what they were feeling or where to put them so they could go home. It could have been Eddie's innate instinct.

Or it could have been something more. Because in the town of Aldermere, that was a possibility.

Morri finished gobbling up the egg. Then she spread her wings and took to the air, flying over Aunt Myrtle's house, referred to as the big house. The raven alighted on the roof, peering toward the middle of town.

"Come on," Fin called after the bird. "We only tried the fetch trick once. I've got another egg."

Morri ignored her. She tilted her head back and forth, fluffed up her feathers indignantly, and then flew toward town.

"Where are you going?" said Fin.

The raven didn't answer, of course.

Eddie shut his textbook and slid off the car. He stared after Morri, a line between his brows. "What is it?" said Fin.

Eddie's frown deepened. "She turned down food. That's weird."

Leaving his homework on the car, Eddie walked around the big house. Fin gave the forgotten textbook and multiplication problems a worried glance. If the wind didn't blow them away, the other ravens might decide to steal them. The birds had a habit of getting into mischief. Hurriedly, Fin picked up the papers, shoved them into Eddie's math book, and crammed it under her arm.

Eddie stood in the front yard. "She flew toward Main Street. What could be more interesting than food?"

Aunt Myrtle's home was on the northwest side of town, where the redwood forest brushed up against the houses and yards. Aldermere was small enough that it only took a few minutes to get to Main Street. Eddie took a shortcut up a gravel alleyway and came out on a sidewalk cracked by tree roots.

"Slow down," called Fin. She still had Eddie's homework under her arm, and sweat trickled down her side. Then she caught sight of the strange car.

A van rolled up Main Street. It was white and orange, with a bright logo printed across the door.

"Is that a—" Eddie began to say.

"Moving van." Fin squinted at it. "I used to see them a lot when I lived down south. We couldn't afford one, and we didn't have enough stuff, anyways. But you'd see them everywhere."

"Moving van," repeated Eddie, mulling over the words. "New neighbors?"

"Or they're trying to find the gas station and got lost," said Fin. Aldermere didn't get a lot of new residents. It was mostly retirees, a few families, and several vacation homes. Not a lot of people wanted to live in the isolation of the Northern California redwoods.

"Let's see." Eddie turned and trotted after the van. It was going slow, as if the occupants weren't used to the rough pavement or the faded street signs. Eddie and Fin passed Mrs. Brackenbury's home. Mrs. Brackenbury herself was dozing on her porch swing, head drooping forward and an audible snore rattling through her nose. Her old bulldog, Mr. Bull, napped between her feet.

The van stopped in the middle of the street, then began to reverse. A man poked his head out of the driver's side window and slowly backed into the driveway of the house beside Mrs. Brackenbury's.

"That's Ben's old place," said Fin. It had been empty for the last six months, after its last occupant was banished from town.

"They must be the new renters," said Eddie.

The passenger door opened with a loud creak. A woman stepped out and smiled at the house. She had brown and gray hair, worn straight down her back in a braid. She was pretty, in a loose blouse and high-waisted jeans. A man got out of the driver's side, squinting through the late afternoon sunlight. He looked a little older—his hair was all gray, with a severe widow's peak. He heaved open the van's sliding door.

A boy leaped down. He had sandy blond hair and black-rimmed glasses, and he wore a blazer unbuttoned over his T-shirt. Unlike the woman, he surveyed the neighborhood the way most people glanced at roadkill.

"Oh no," whispered Eddie. He seized Fin by the elbow, dragging her down behind the wooden fence. Fin wobbled and nearly fell onto her knees.

"What are you doing?" asked Fin. She clutched Eddie's textbook so it wouldn't fall into Mrs. Brackenbury's daffodils. Luckily, Mrs. Brackenbury was still asleep.

"It can't be," said Eddie, peering through the slats of the fence. "River." He said the name in the same tone she'd once heard him use for "I found moldy dishes beneath my bed."

River was a . . . Fin thought the right word was "rival" but Eddie would've said "archnemesis" or something equally dramatic. As long as Fin had known him, Eddie had only ever held a grudge against one person. River and Eddie were opposites in every way: Eddie loved animals and nature; River loved technology and the indoors. When Eddie brought lizards to the science fair, River brought a functioning Popsicle-stick windmill that actually made electricity.

"He is *not* moving here," said Eddie. "This is my town. He does not get to—no!"

Because at that moment, the woman had gone around to the back of the van and opened it, pulling out a box labeled KITCHEN. She handed the box to River, who began lugging it toward the front door.

"No, no, no," murmured Eddie. His fingers tightened on the wooden slats of the fence. He watched as River struggled to maneuver the heavy box through the front door. "Go ask if they're the new renters."

"What?" said Fin, startled. "Why me?"

Fin was anxious. And not in the "sometimes I'm worried about things" way. In the "I have a diagnosis, a counselor, and a lot of coping techniques" way. And while she had been working on her anxiety, she didn't relish the idea of walking up to River and his family to demand if they were moving in.

"Come on, please," said Eddie. "I can't do it—River hates me."

Fin pressed a hand to her eyes. "Fine. But I'm going to the coffee shop and getting some muffins or something as a welcoming gift. And you're taking this." She held out his math textbook.

"You just want Cedar to come with you," said Eddie.

"Of course I do," said Fin, unashamed.

"All right," said Eddie. "I'll meet you at the inn afterward. Mom wanted me to check and see if she needed to deliver more postcards to the front desk." With a furtive look over his shoulder, Eddie hurried off in the direction of the inn.

Aldermere's coffee shop, Brewed Awakening, was across the street from Mrs. Brackenbury's home. There were a few tables out front, all of them occupied by people chatting over drinks. The inside always smelled like old wood, ground coffee, and fresh pastries.

Fin pushed open the door and scooted past a few tourists. There were three indoor tables, and Cedar sat at the farthest one. She had straight dark hair, cut into a short bob that made her look like an old-time movie star. This week her nails were painted a delicate shade of turquoise. "Hey," she said, smiling when she saw Fin.

"I need a partner in crime," said Fin apologetically. Fin and Cedar had known each other since Fin moved to Aldermere three and a half years before, but they hadn't become friends until last fall. Fin had accidentally created a doppelgänger out of forgotten memories and tea. Cedar had helped Fin with that situation. It made them fast friends.

Cedar shut her book. "Okay." She stepped behind the

counter. "Hey, Dad—Fin and I are going for a walk."

Mr. Carver was behind the counter, using a pair of tongs to slide a bagel into a paper bag. He'd rolled up his sleeves, revealing intricate tattoos on both forearms. He had the same light brown skin and straight dark hair as Cedar—the same easy smile too. Fin liked him.

"You two have a good time," he said, then turned back to the customer.

"Wait." Fin rummaged around in her pocket. "I need to buy cookies or something."

"Crime requires cookies?" asked Cedar, a laugh in her voice.

"Unfortunately," said Fin.

Cedar ducked behind the counter again, emerging with a bag of pretty pink pastries. "We've got some conchas."

"Those'll be perfect." Fin found a five-dollar bill. It had been a cash tip from one of her deliveries. Cedar caught sight of the money and shook her head.

"It's fine," she said. "You can buy us ice cream later."

This was one of the things Fin liked about Cedar— she understood the delicate balance of favors. Fin was keenly aware of *owing* people, and it always made her feel itchy and uncomfortable when the scales weren't balanced. Eddie would have wondered why Fin felt the need to pay Cedar back, but Cedar understood.

Together they walked out of the coffee shop. Fin explained on the way, and Cedar's face sharpened with understanding. "Scott River is moving here?"

"Wait, River's his last name?" said Fin.

"Yeah," said Cedar. "You didn't know?"

"He's a grade ahead of me," said Fin, shrugging. "And I've only ever heard Eddie refer to him as River."

"I think it's because River started calling Eddie Edward," said Cedar. "And we all know how he feels about that."

The moving van came into view. All its doors were open, and a man was hefting another box out of the back. Fin hesitated on the sidewalk; then she took a breath and walked up the driveway. The man—who must have been Mr. River, Fin thought—saw them and nodded a greeting before putting the box on the small porch.

"Hello there," he said.

"Hi," said Cedar brightly. "I'm Cedar, and this is Fin."

Fin said, "We saw you moving in and wanted to say welcome to Aldermere!" She held out the bag of conchas. "You eat gluten, hopefully?"

Mr. River laughed and took the proffered bag. "Yes, all of us. And thank you—you're both very sweet. Fin and . . . what was your name again?"

"Cedar," said Cedar. "We both go to school with Scott."

Mr. River's smile broadened. "Ah, that makes sense. Let me get him for you, then." Before either of them could protest, Mr. River picked up the box and strode inside the house. Fin could hear the low murmur of voices, then River himself slunk through the open door.

He was a little taller than Fin—almost Cedar's height. His dark-rimmed glasses had slipped down his nose, and there was a cobweb snagged on his sleeve. He caught sight of them and scowled. "You're Edward's sister, aren't you?"

"His cousin," said Fin. "Fin. And you know Cedar, right?"

River's eyes darted to Cedar before returning to Fin. "Did he send you here?"

Not long ago, Fin would have shrunk beneath such a glare. But now she held her shoulders straight. She'd been meeting with a counselor twice a month since September, and some of the lessons came back to her. *Just because a person is angry doesn't mean it's your fault.*

"We were bringing your family a gift," said Fin, mentally crossing her fingers behind her back.

If anything, this irritated River more. "We're not staying here, you know," he said. "This . . . this is a temporary thing. You can tell Edward that."

"Oh," said Cedar. "Well, if you need anything—"

"I'll ask someone else," said River, turning on his heel. He walked, stiff legged, inside the house and shut the door.

"That was rude," said Cedar.

"I think that's his default setting," said Fin. "His dad seemed nice. Wonder why River's such a jerk."

Cedar shrugged. "Sometimes kids go through things without their parents noticing," she said evenly.

Like accidentally creating a tea doppelgänger, Fin thought to herself.

"Well, we can tell Eddie the news, at least," Fin said aloud. "He'll be glad to hear they aren't staying forever."

"And Brewed Awakening's logo is on the bag we gave them," said Cedar, brightening. "So if his parents drink coffee, we may drum up two new customers."

Fin took a step back, turning away from River's house. "I'm going to meet Eddie at the inn. You want to come?"

"Sure." Cedar fell into step beside her. "I don't have much homework. And I've got a week to do it. You got any plans for spring break?"

Fin had plans—but she wasn't sure anyone else would consider them Plans with a capital P. She was looking forward to a week's worth of quiet: of reading a few old mystery books, watching Eddie play video games, and trying to teach Morri to play fetch.

"Not really," she replied. "You?"

Cedar shrugged. "There'll be a lot of tourists in town, so my parents might need help at the Foragers' Market. But nothing else. I was thinking maybe a hike, if you were interested?"

"Sounds good."

They walked up Main Street toward the inn. Aldermere had done its best to look welcoming for its spring-break visitors: people had trimmed their lawns and made sure that front-facing windows were clean, and some had even set out little lawn decorations that looked like the traditional Bigfoot or a flying saucer.

The inn was by far the biggest building in town—and the biggest employer. Fin's mother was the assistant manager, and Fin spent a lot of time at the inn. Sometimes she helped her mom, folding napkins or moving chairs, or sometimes she just hung out in her mom's office.

As was usual this time of year, most of the parking spaces were filled. Tourists tended to flock to the Redwood Highway during spring and summer, eager for hikes and camping and a beautiful—if slightly nauseating, thanks to all the curvy roads—road trip.

Eddie was lurking beside an oversized truck. He crouched, peering around the large tire. Fin let out a sigh.

"What poor person are you spying on now?"

"Not a person," said Eddie. "That." He pointed over the truck's bed, and Fin caught sight of a new van near the edge of the parking lot.

It was large—but that was where all similarities to River's moving van ended. This van was built for adventure. It had a squat, sturdy look, and there was a metal rack atop it, heavy with camera equipment. The van had been painted in a camouflage swirl of muted greens and grays. SOCIETY OF NORTH AMERICAN CRYPTID CHASERS was printed in bright orange letters. Each of the words had a bolded first letter that made the entire thing look like SNACC.

Three strangers were unloading equipment. Their shoes were untouched by dirt and their T-shirts all bore the same orange-and-green logo. A young man with dark skin and curly hair wore what looked like a shoulder holster with two cameras dangling beneath each arm. A second man had blond hair and carried a laptop bag. And the last person was a pale woman with green hair shaved close on one side and longer on the other. She appeared to be directing the others as they gathered their belongings. Fin wasn't great with guessing adults' ages, but she put them somewhere in their twenties.

"What's SNACC?" said Fin.

"Something you eat between lunch and dinner," said Eddie, grinning.

Cedar frowned at the strangers. "I know them."

"You've met them before?" asked Fin.

Cedar made a vague gesture in the direction of the coffee shop. "No, but I know *of* them. You know how my parents were into bigfoot hunting?"

"But they gave it up," said Fin.

Cedar nodded. "Yeah. But they still know others in the business. The Society of North American Cryptid Chasers got in touch a year ago to ask for an interview. The woman— that's Ana Bell. She's debunked a lot of stuff. I think she was doing some spotlights on older cryptid hunters. She found one of Mom's old books. But Mom turned them down, said they'd retired."

"Ah, so SNACC's into cryptography," said Eddie knowledgeably.

"Crypto*zoology*," said Cedar. "Cryptography's something else."

"What is it then?" asked Eddie, his forehead wrinkling in thought.

"Codes, I think," said Cedar. "Or maybe mapmaking."

"Hey," said Fin, resisting the urge to wave her hands at them. "Did you say they debunk stuff?"

"Yeah." Cedar ran a hand through her dark hair. "They've visited places where gravity is supposedly upended and water runs uphill. In Los Angeles, they tested some animal fur that was supposed to belong to a squirroose. It turned out to be opossum hair."

Fin snorted. "What's a squirroose?"

"Half squirrel, half moose," said Eddie.

For a moment, Fin brought to mind a giant squirrel with antlers, then a tiny moose climbing trees and stealing snacks from tourists. Both were equally horrifying.

"Squirrooses don't exist," said Cedar. "At least, I don't think so."

Fin gazed at the van, and her stomach sank. The strangers were headed inside the inn, carrying luggage and glancing around Aldermere with intent. "You know what this means, right?" said Fin.

"That I'm never going to meet a squirroose?" said Eddie.

"They're here," said Fin, "for Aldermere."

TWO
An Unexpected Meeting

Aldermere was a small town in Northern California surrounded by an old-growth redwood forest. It was a stop along Highway 101 where long-haul road trippers could get a room at the inn, stop for coffee, or wander one of the many hiking trails.

It was also a hot spot for weirdness. Those seeking Bigfoot or aliens often came to town—and when they left, they carried redwood needles wrapped with twine ("magic tree needles," read the hand-written label), plush toy mice with too many legs (they squeaked if their stomach was squeezed), and postcards of watercolor redwood forests (painted by Fin's aunt Myrtle). Aldermere had seized upon its reputation for strange happenings, using it to merchandise and draw in tourists that might have driven by. Most of the visitors came for a selfie and a laugh.

But here was a truth hidden in plain sight: magic was real. And it existed only in and around Aldermere. It wasn't the kind of magic that Fin had read about when she was younger. There were no spells, no waving of wands or chants. The rules were whispered from local to local, never written down.

Doors must be labeled or they can lead anywhere.

Pay the ravens or keep your garbage bins inside.

Never keep a knife that's tasted your blood.

Always drop a bread crust into Bower's Creek before going into the water.

Don't use the old toll bridge north of town—there is a price, but no one knows what it is.

Burn nothing within the town borders.

There were other unspoken oddities: the deer of Aldermere cast unsettling shadows, the tea shop had a tendency to vanish (and thanks to Fin, it hadn't been found in six months), and strange creatures lived both in and around Aldermere.

Aldermere was unsettling and eerie . . . and wonderful. Despite all its quirks—or perhaps because of them—Fin loved the small town. It was the first place she'd ever thought of as home. Magic wasn't good or bad. It was a force of nature. You couldn't change it or control it—you learned how to live with it.

That night Aldermere held an emergency town meeting.

Normally town meetings were on Mondays, but this one wasn't official—for one thing, it was held in Mrs. Brackenbury's living room. It would've been awkward to hold it at the inn, where the film crew might wander by.

Fin had been to Mrs. Brackenbury's home several times. The elderly lady was friendly and talkative, often sitting on her porch with her lumpy bulldog, Mr. Bull. She had lived alone until Talia moved in six months ago. Which, Fin reflected with a twinge of guilt, was her fault. Talia had owned and lived in the tea shop. When someone had tried to steal the magic inside, Fin had defended it the only way she could: by making it vanish. Talia was confident that she would find her tea shop one day, but it had yet to reappear.

Mrs. Brackenbury was waving people into her home. "Finley! So nice to see you. And Angelina, you're looking well. Eddie, Myrtle," she said, squeezing Aunt Myrtle's hand. "I'm so glad you came."

"Of course," said Aunt Myrtle. "Someone has to keep the mayor from being . . . well, herself."

"I heard it was mandatory for all business managers," said Fin's mom.

Mom and her older sister, Myrtle, were a study in contrasts: Aunt Myrtle had long brown hair, streaked with gray at the temples. Her clothes were breezy and comfortable, and an assortment of necklaces fell into her blouse. She made her living by selling her artwork and doing tarot readings for tourists at the Foragers' Market. Mom had the same brown hair, but hers was shoulder length and dyed to cover any gray. She wore makeup, black slacks, and a crisp white shirt—which meant she'd come straight from the inn.

"Not so much mandatory," hedged Mrs. Brackenbury, "as highly encouraged by our esteemed mayor. I think she's worried that people will close up shop, so she wants to remind us not to be unwelcoming."

Aunt Myrtle snorted. "I don't see what all the fuss is about. So some amateur film people are at the inn. It's not the first time."

"I think it's cool," said Eddie.

"So they *are* here to study Aldermere?" said Fin. Normally, she wouldn't have spoken up amid so many people—but it was something she'd been working on. Her words came out a little rushed, but they were understandable.

Mrs. Brackenbury shrugged. "That's what we're going to

find out, I suppose." Another group of townspeople walked up the porch steps and she waved at them, gesturing Fin and her family inside. "Go on, go on. There're fresh snickerdoodle cookies in the kitchen."

The house was comfortably cluttered with old knickknacks and pictures. The living room was already crowded; the loveseat was claimed by a few of the town elders, and the recliner was guarded—or rather, napped in— by Mr. Bull himself. He was so old that Mrs. Brackenbury had to put him in a stroller for long walks.

"Come on, I want a cookie," said Eddie, tugging on Fin's jacket. She followed him, grateful for a reason not to talk to anyone.

Mom and Aunt Myrtle found a place to stand beside Frank, a lumberjack/handyman/wildlife tracker with a thick dark beard and quiet demeanor. A white ferret nestled in his hooded sweatshirt, eyes closed as it slept. Beside him, narrowly eyeing the ferret, was Cassandra Catmore, the editor of the *Aldermere Oracle*. She had a pencil tucked behind one ear and another between her fingers. Petra Petrichor had claimed a space near the front door, her hawkish gaze sweeping over the crowd. She was the head of the volunteer firefighters, unofficial arson investigator, and the closest thing Aldermere had to a sheriff. Also in attendance were

Mr. Madeira, the Reyes family, Mr. Hardin from the grocery store, and several other familiar faces.

Talia stood in a far corner, watching people bustle through the room. She had gray hair, keen eyes, and perfectly neat orange-red lipstick. When she saw Fin, she held up a hand in greeting. Fin nodded back.

Finally Mrs. Brackenbury stepped inside and locked the door behind her. It seemed a rather ominous way to begin a meeting. Fin and Eddie lingered in the doorway between the living room and kitchen, each holding a cookie.

"Order! Order, please!"

The mayor of Aldermere climbed atop a wooden chair. Mayor Downer was a solidly built woman with a square jaw and a stare that could pierce a rulebreaker at twenty feet.

"Order," she repeated, and Fin had the distinct impression that Mayor Downer wished she had a gavel to rap. "Quiet down, everyone."

The hum of conversation died down to a few scattered whispers. Mrs. Brackenbury reclaimed her recliner, situating Mr. Bull on her lap. Mayor Downer waited another five seconds, then drew in a breath. "Some of you know why this meeting was called."

"Mrs. Brackenbury's baking?" murmured someone on the other side of the room.

"Oh, hush," said Mrs. Brackenbury, but she was beaming.

"First things first," said Mayor Downer. She looked around the room, meeting several people's gazes. "There's a prescribed burn happening about twenty miles northeast, so if you see smoke on the horizon, do not call the fire department. Cal Fire is trying to clear out some of the brush before fire season starts. Also, there have been a few reports of hikers leaving food out on trails. If you see abandoned picnics, please help clean them up before we have a bear problem again.

"And on to our most important piece of business," continued Mayor Downer. "If you don't know, a group calling themselves the Society for . . ." She checked a notecard— an *actual* paper notecard—and said, "Northern American Cryptid Chasers is in town. They're filming a new episode for their"—another glance at the notecard—"internet web series."

"Why can't we just chase them out of town like we did with the ghost hunters five years ago?" said Mr. Madeira.

Eddie nudged Fin with his elbow. "I remember that," he said in an undertone. "They heard a rumor someone drowned in one of the water towers, so they thought it might be haunted."

"Was it?" murmured Fin.

Eddie took a bite of his cookie and grinned. "Sure. By a family of raccoons."

Mayor Downer pinched the bridge of her nose, as if gathering her patience. "We didn't chase anyone out of town. They left when they didn't find anything."

"They did buy several of my paintings, though," said Aunt Myrtle brightly.

"The point is," said Mayor Downer, "we cannot let this opportunity pass."

"What do you mean, opportunity?" asked Mrs. Petrichor.

Mayor Downer squared her shoulders. "This . . . ah, *documentary* would provide the town with some good publicity."

There was a moment of surprised quiet—as if people were trying to figure out who should speak up. Then Mr. Madeira said, "You think the publicity would bring in more tourists?"

"Precisely," said Mayor Downer.

"Who needs more?" said Mr. Hardin, owner of Aldermere Grocery & Tackle. "The inn is at capacity, right?" He glanced at Fin's mom.

"We are currently full," Mom said, with a certain amount of pride. "We had to turn away a few hikers this afternoon."

Mayor Downer made a *tsk*ing sound with her tongue.

"It's spring break," she said. "Of course it's crowded. And come summer, we'll be busy again. But we have to think about the off-season. And the last few years, we've begun to get fewer tourists during the late summer months due to smoke. We don't get nearly enough visitors—"

"You want more people to visit during fire season?" said Mrs. Petrichor sharply. "Do you realize how dangerous that could be for any evacuation plans?"

Mayor Downer shook her head. "All right, perhaps not then—"

"Mayor Downer wants tourists to burn," muttered Aunt Myrtle in a none-too-quiet tone. She nudged Ms. Catmore. "Make sure that's a headline."

Ms. Catmore's pencil flashed across her notepad.

Mayor Downer's patience began to unravel. "Order, please!"

"What about the magic?" asked Frank. He had a rasp of a voice, low and rough. "We can't have them filming it."

"Sure we can," said Mr. Hardin. "What are they going to film? It's not like they know what to look for. I'll make sure the store cat chases any whintossers away and as long as the ravens get their weekly tribute, they'll keep to themselves." He shrugged. "These people make a living disproving the supernatural, right? Then we make this place look as cheap and corny as they'd expect. Sell them snow globes with redwoods in them. Put out the signs that say Bigfoot Crossing. Do a tarot reading—"

"Hey," said Aunt Myrtle, a bit miffed. "My readings are not cheap."

"—and then they can walk away feeling superior," finished Mr. Hardin. "They'll post some episode about how Aldermere is an undiscovered vacation spot. No sign of weird stuff anywhere. There's no need for panicking or hiding."

Mayor Downer tipped her head in acknowledgment. "That's a fair plan." She glanced around the room. "Everyone, just remember to make sure to feed the ravens. And double-check your door labels. We'll get some good publicity, and the town will be safe."

"Perhaps," said a quiet, firm voice, "but those filmmakers might not be."

All eyes in the room turned toward the front door. Someone had come in without anyone noticing—and how he'd managed with the locked door, Fin had no idea. He had dark hair, a nose that looked as if it had been broken a few times, and deep-set eyes. He looked a little like an old guard dog, battle scarred and tired, but still formidable.

Nicodemus Elphinstone—or Nick, as everyone called

him—never came to town meetings. As a rule, he didn't even come into town. In three and a half years, Fin had only seen him cross the boundary into Aldermere once. No one knew why. Some people said it was because Nick had done something to anger the magic; others claimed it was because he couldn't stand some of the town's inhabitants; others thought the ravens had a vendetta against him—but considering Nick's affinity for the birds, Fin doubted that last one.

A hush fell across the room, punctuated by a few sharp inhalations.

Mayor Downer's expression changed. It was like watching a computer lose power—all the light and life drained from her face, leaving her emptier and scarier than Fin had ever seen.

"You," said Mayor Downer, her voice quietly seething, "are not welcome here."

The tension of the room drew taut, ready to snap. At once, Fin wanted to shrink into the kitchen, where no one could see her. It didn't matter if the argument had nothing to do with her—Fin's old instincts screamed at her to retreat and hide. She forced herself to stay still, to take a deep breath and watch.

"This is not an opportunity," said Nick quietly. "It is a

risk. Tell me, what will happen when these filmmakers find something that can't be explained? Not all that dwell within the forest can be as easily chased away as a few whintossers or ravens." He turned, meeting the eyes of several people nearby. "What happens if they stumble into Bower's Creek? Or if one of them goes missing in the woods?"

An uneasy murmur rippled through the crowd. "And what would your solution be?" said Mayor Downer, making no effort to hide her scorn. "Tell them the truth?"

Nick shook his head. "Make them leave," he said simply. "Tell them their rooms at the inn are double-booked."

"I'm not risking the inn's reputation like that," said Fin's mom firmly. Her voice startled Fin; Mom almost never spoke during meetings. She preferred to watch and listen while sipping a cup of coffee. "They're paying customers. And we can't afford bad reviews, especially not from anyone influential."

Fin glanced from her mom to Nick, torn between them. The truth was, she didn't know which side she was on. Mom was right that the inn needed guests—tourism was Aldermere's beating heart, the way most businesses stayed afloat. The only reason Fin could even stay in Aldermere was because Mom worked at the inn. If all that went away, she would have to leave. And that thought scared her more than anything else.

But Fin also knew what happened when people tried to profit from magic.

It drove the magic away.

"If you're not willing to offend a few customers, we risk something worse than bad reviews," said Nick.

"What risk are you talking about?" said Mayor Downer sharply.

"People cannot defend themselves from something they don't believe exists," said Nick. "Hikers keep to the trails and know how to conduct themselves in the wilderness. But do you think *these* people will confine themselves to trails?" He tucked his hands behind his back, shoulders straight. "We know of the town's dangers. We have learned to navigate them. But these people are here to dig, to unearth secrets, to go into the forest looking for myths to unravel. In all likelihood, they won't find anything. But what if something finds *them*?"

And with those heavy words, he turned on his heel and walked out Mrs. Brackenbury's front door.

THREE
Things in the Forest

"**W**ell, now I get why Nick doesn't come to town council meetings," said Fin. She sat amid a chaotic jumble of boxes and packing paper, a small wooden painting in her hands. Morning sunlight cut through the big house's dining room window, illuminating motes of dust. "Mayor Downer really doesn't like him."

"Mayor Downer doesn't like anyone," said Eddie. He was taping a box shut; the squeal of packing tape nearly drowned out his words. He checked to make sure the box was securely shut, then nodded in satisfaction.

Aunt Myrtle had an art show south, in Mendocino. Helping her aunt hadn't been part of Fin's spring break plans, but when she'd emerged from the cottage she and her mother shared, Aunt Myrtle had waved her toward the big house, pressed a roll of tape into Fin's hands, and said, "Come on, we've got work to do." Fin didn't mind; there was something almost soothing in the repetition of taking paintings, wrapping them in paper, and carefully putting them in boxes that Eddie enthusiastically taped up. They worked at the dining room table—which was actually an old door fashioned into a table. Fin could see the dents and nicks from over the years, smoothed over with polish.

"Yeah, but she *hated* Nick," said Fin. She picked up another small painting; this one was of redwood needles on a forest floor. She began wrapping it in brown paper. "Maybe that's why he doesn't come into town."

"Because Mayor Downer has it in for him?" Eddie snorted, brandishing the tape dispenser at Fin. "If that's the case, then my mom would've had to move out years ago. I think they've had more fights."

"Who's had more fights?" asked Aunt Myrtle brightly as she walked into the dining room.

"You and Mayor Downer," said Eddie.

Aunt Myrtle flicked her fingers as if brushing away an irritating fly. "Oh, her. We don't fight . . . we have different opinions. Loudly." She hefted two more boxes into her arms and ambled outside.

"How long will she be gone for?" asked Fin.

"Her art opening is tomorrow," said Eddie. "Then she'll spend a few days in Mendocino to see old friends. I think she's coming back on Thursday."

"Why aren't you going with her?" asked Fin. She handed him a painting, and he put it into the box with the others.

Eddie shrugged. "She offered, but honestly Highway One always makes me carsick. And it'll just be her and her art friends. More fun to stay here."

After Fin taped up the last of the paintings, she slipped out of the kitchen and made for the cottage.

Fin and her mother lived in an A-frame cottage about fifty feet behind the big house. It used to be a vacation home Aunt Myrtle rented to tourists. It was small, with mostly secondhand furniture, and it could get drafty—but Fin loved it. She loved the tiny wood stove, the kitchen with its windows that overlooked a patch of ferns, the redwood forest only a few steps away, and the way the light shone through the window in her upstairs bedroom. Her loft had built-in bookshelves crowded with old paperback mysteries, and her bed was made up with soft flannel sheets and an old crocheted blanket from

Fin's grandmother. The one thing the cottage lacked was internet.

When Fin wanted to get online, she hauled the old family laptop into the big house or the backyard. The wireless network's password was Eddie's birthday, which at least made it easy to log on. While Eddie helped Aunt Myrtle load up her car, Fin dragged one of the folding lawn chairs toward the big house's back porch within reach of the Wi-Fi.

Fin opened up the web browser and typed in a search. "Society of North American Cryptic," because the computer's autocorrect didn't recognize "cryptid." Luckily the internet figured it out.

When their website loaded, a logo flashed across the screen, identical to the one painted across the van. It did look like SNACC, which undercut the feeling of dread in Fin's stomach. It was hard to be afraid of something that sounded like a meal. Thirty-five videos had been posted, each about thirty minutes long. The series dedicated one to three episodes to a single local legend—although they had spent five episodes on something called a chupacabra. Curious, Fin clicked to the very first episode. It wasn't about a creature at all, but a mystery spot farther south.

"For those of you who enjoy the feeling of being

off-balance, who tell stories at night about the ghost that once haunted your grandmother's kitchen, who believe that throwing salt over your shoulder might protect you from bad luck," said the green-haired young woman, "I suggest you stop watching." She had a wicked curve to her smile. "But for those of you who wish to see how things work, to understand the world around you all the better . . . please enjoy."

Ana Bell, Fin remembered. That was what Cedar had called her.

Ana Bell had a presence—her dark eyes seemed to draw the camera closer; she spoke with both authority and a wit that made a person want to listen; her dyed hair made her striking. She spoke of the history of mystery spots, of local attractions that were developed as families began to travel by car, and of several famous places across America. And then she stepped inside a crooked house and had to stand in a way that made it look as though gravity were askew.

"Why am I currently leaning so far to one side?" asked Ana with a little smile. "For the same reason that my cameraman refuses to come inside. Tell us, Michael."

A male voice came from behind the camera. "I can't brace myself against a wall and hold a camera," the voice said wryly. "The whole house is tilted."

Ana nodded. "Exactly. These so-called gravity houses are an optical illusion. Everything's at a twenty-degree angle, which tilts the person as well. But don't take my word for it." The scene cut to an interview with a college professor who explained how people's perceptions could be deceived by shifting things even a little.

Fin watched, fascinated. By the end, she was wholly convinced that mystery spots were hoaxes . . . even though she *believed* in magic. Fin clicked through several more episodes, watching a few minutes of each. There was a narrative threaded through the videos—the story of Ana Bell and her twin brother, Ryan. Their cameraman, Michael, had been Ryan's college roommate. The three of them were a team, tracing the roots of local myths and urban legends.

The SNACC Pack, Fin thought as she scrolled over a picture of Ana, Ryan, and Michael standing in front of their iconic van.

Seeing the show made everything both better and worse. Better, because it was clear the show was more about disproving magic than finding it. But worse, because Fin saw their subscriber numbers. Hundreds of thousands of people watched those videos. If Ana Bell and her team managed to find something unexplainable, it would be right on camera, for all the world to see.

Which meant they *couldn't* find anything. Fin, and the rest of Aldermere, had to make sure of it.

Fin's mom was in the kitchen when Fin walked inside, laptop tucked under her arm. Mom wore red oven mitts, and her hair was pulled into a bun.

"Myrtle done using you as free labor?" said Mom, but she was smiling. She pulled a frittata out of the oven, setting it onto the coils of their stove. Steam billowed into the air, fogging up the kitchen's only window. Mom hung the oven mitts on a hook near the fridge.

"Her car's all packed up," said Fin, setting the laptop on a bookshelf. "Is Eddie going to stay here while she's gone, or are we going to sleep at the big house?"

On the occasions that Aunt Myrtle went out of town or Mom had to work a night shift, Eddie and Fin would sleep over at either the big house or the cottage. More often, it was the big house. Eddie's upstairs bedroom might be messy, and occasionally an animal would find its way inside, but he also had a gaming computer and they could bunk on the floor with sleeping bags and a camping lantern. Aunt Myrtle and Mom were under the impression that two kids would get into less trouble if they were together . . . and neither Fin nor Eddie had ever mentioned some of the things that had gone awry during those nights. Like accidentally summoning a tea monster.

"Eddie will stay here," said Mom. "Frank's stopping by the big house tomorrow to take a look at the roof." She cut a triangle of the frittata and slid it onto a plate. She was a good cook, but the inn kept her too busy for elaborate meals.

Fin's mouth watered at the scents of potatoes and fresh herbs. "This looks good."

"It's a new recipe," said Mom. She set one plate before Fin, then picked up her own. Their table was small, just big enough for two. Mom had made it her mission to eat at least one meal a day with Fin since last fall, and while Fin sometimes rolled her eyes at Mom's insisting they sit down for scrambled eggs or instant oatmeal, she enjoyed it.

"How's the inn?" asked Fin.

"Full up. We've got a lot of spring breakers this year. A few families hiking the new trail south. And the film crew, of course."

"What do you think about them?" asked Fin, using the edge of her fork to saw off a piece of frittata.

Mom ate delicately with her knife and fork. "I think it's a lot of fuss for no reason. They're just people with cameras and a van. We get people looking for magic all the time. These ones have been quiet and tipped the cleaners decently, so I have no problem with the Society of Crypto—something or other."

"SNACC," said Fin.

Mom raised one eyebrow. "Finish brunch, then we'll talk."

"No," said Fin. "S-N-A-C-C. The film crew's logo looks like SNACC. It's easier to remember."

Mom let out a startled laugh. "SNACC," she said. "All right." She took another bite, swallowed, then said, "And what do you think of them?"

Fin shrugged. "I don't know. I think Eddie's more excited than I am."

"Well," said Mom, "I'm sure they won't find anything . . . unusual."

Mom almost never uttered the word "magic." Maybe it was because she distrusted the magic or because she'd been led astray by it—but she always kept the strangeness at a distance.

"So," said Mom, as if she needed to change the subject. "What are your plans for spring break?"

Fin considered. "I have a book report to write. And some math homework to finish. I want to get those done today, so I don't have to think about it for the rest of the week."

"And other than homework?" Mom collected the plates and walked them to the sink.

"Cedar wants to go on a hike," said Fin. "And Eddie will probably try to spy on River."

Mom chuckled. "Those two." She finished washing the plates, setting them in the rack. Then she leaned her hip against the counter, looking at Fin. It was a look that Fin had come to know over the years: evaluating. Before, it might have made Fin shrink back and glance away because it felt like an examination, like Mom was looking for something wrong. But now Fin told herself it was just Mom considering her.

"You know," said Mom, "if you get bored, we've got some brochures at the inn that need folding."

"No offense," said Fin, "but I hope my spring break isn't that boring."

Mom laughed and kissed the crown of Fin's head. "None taken. Tell Eddie to bring his toothbrush over tonight, and anything else he needs. I'll be home by nine. You two should be in the loft by then."

"Eddie's still trying to teach me to play cards," said Fin. "And I want to finish my homework. So I don't think that'll be a problem."

"And you said the inn was boring," said Mom. She picked up her jacket and house keys, leaving the cottage. Fin watched her go, still smiling.

✦ ✦ ✦

That afternoon Aunt Myrtle waved farewell to Fin and Eddie through the window of her car. They waved dutifully back as she turned toward Highway 101 and then vanished from sight. Once she was gone, they took their homework to the cottage porch. There was an old rocking chair where Fin liked to sit, and Eddie sprawled on the overgrown grass. He would've gone into the woods, but Fin firmly refused until she got her homework done. He grudgingly went along with that, his pencil wedged between his teeth as he watched a moth flutter through the air.

When Fin had finished her book report, she went inside for drinks. Eddie was poking at a math problem, his pencil eraser beating out a steady rhythm against his textbook. "Some Saturday," he said, accepting the cup of orange juice. "First packing boxes and now homework."

"If I don't get this done now, I'll procrastinate," said Fin. "Then I'll worry about time running out, even as I'm not doing it." Starting something was often like trying to climb a hill; if she didn't start immediately, it grew into an unclimbable mountain.

"How's the counseling stuff going?" asked Eddie. "You think it's helping?"

"Yes," said Fin. "I mean, sort of. We're talking stuff out.

My counselor is giving me ways to deal with the thoughts. But they still come back." She sat down on the grass beside him. A ladybug crawled across her ankle. "She said when I'm a little older, there are medications I can try."

"You think you will?" asked Eddie, curious. He was one of those people who never seemed to worry. It seemed like a superpower.

But one thing Fin liked about her cousin was that even though he didn't understand her anxiety, he never judged her for it.

Fin shrugged. "Don't know yet." That would be a decision for Future Fin. In the meantime, the counseling sessions were good for understanding her own anxieties, even if it didn't make them disappear. Only magic could do that. But Fin had tried that—and it hadn't ended well.

That night, Fin jolted awake.

Everything was dark and still. Redwood forests had a way of muffling sound; the fallen needles softened every footfall. At first it had made Fin uncomfortable, but she'd grown used to the quiet.

But this was different. It wasn't the silence of a peaceful forest, but that of a held breath.

Moonlight cascading through the window illuminated

Eddie's still form. His sleeping bag was on the floor, and he had one arm sprawled out, his face slack with sleep. Whatever had woken Fin clearly hadn't roused him.

She frowned and cast a look at her alarm clock. It was three in the morning. She should have gone back to sleep, but unease prickled along her skin.

The window was open. And something deep within Fin—an old instinct, one that made all kids close their closet doors and never look under their beds at night—knew that she should close it.

One did not leave windows open at the witching hour.

Fin put one bare foot against the floor. So she felt it when the whole house *trembled.*

Dust fell from an overhead rafter, and the cup of water by Fin's bed shivered.

Fin's stomach lurched. *An earthquake,* she thought.

But if it was an earthquake, it had been faint. And no one in California blinked at anything less than a five-pointer.

Still. Fin should close the window.

She stepped from her bed, careful in case the house shook a second time. She picked her way around Eddie and to the window. The moon was full, illuminating a cloudless sky and painting the tree branches in silver. Fin froze with her hands on the windowsill.

It wasn't an earthquake.

Something was moving in the forest.

She could hear it—the low thud of footsteps, the rustle of ferns, and the creak of trees.

It couldn't be the wind; the night air was still.

Fin leaned on the sill, trying to peer through the darkness. Even the bright moonlight couldn't slip through the thick boughs to the forest floor.

Her gaze strained through the dark as she gazed at the woods, trying to see—

Something stepped out of the tree line. A shadow. Four legged and large.

For a moment, Fin thought it must be a deer. The deer of Aldermere looked normal, except for their shadows. Their shadows were too big, their horns too broad, and they had arms that looked unsettlingly human.

But this shadow couldn't belong to a deer, Fin realized.

Because it wasn't *attached to anything*.

The formless darkness looked a little like a horse. But while Fin had always liked looking at horses, this creature made her insides go cold.

The creature glanced from side to side, shook its head,

then walked into the yard. Fin tensed. She leaned out the open window, gaze tracking the creature as it approached the big house.

Hastily, Fin knelt beside Eddie and gave him a shake. He groaned in his sleep.

"Wake up," she whispered. Her throat was dry and tight. "Something's out there."

Eddie mumbled a protest and rolled over.

There was no time to wake him.

Fin stepped over Eddie, darting to her loft's ladder. She descended as quickly as she could and hurried into the kitchen, where a window looked out toward the big house. Her heart thudded against her ribs as she rose to tiptoe, leaning over the countertop. She could only just make out the shape of the creature.

She expected to see it trying to break into the big house. But the shadow creature merely sniffed at the back door before trotting around the corner and vanishing from sight.

Fin stood there for several minutes, until her heartbeat calmed and she was sure the creature wouldn't reappear. She checked to make sure the door was locked, then climbed the ladder back to her loft. Eddie was drooling into his pillow. She would tell him in the morning, Fin decided.

Fin was used to Aldermere's cryptids: the small, mouse-like whintossers with their too-many legs, the ravens with their all-knowing gazes and weekly tribute, the deer with their monstrous shadows, and the unseen thing in Bower's Creek. And Fin was used to the normal wildlife—the cougars and bears that occasionally wandered close to town. They were familiar, and so long as a person knew how to deal with them, they weren't dangerous.

But she had never seen anything like that creature. And no one had ever spoken of such a thing. Surely, if there were shadow monsters near Aldermere, the townspeople would know about them.

She climbed back into bed, drawing the covers up to her chin.

And tried not to think about how easily a shadow could slip through the night.

FOUR
Leave Only Footprints

*R*ap-rap-rap.

Fin jerked awake to the sound of knocking. "Morri?" she said groggily.

"Mmrf." Eddie rolled over, pulling his pillow over his head.

Fin looked to the window. The raven was nowhere in sight.

The knocking came a second time—and Fin realized the sound was coming from the front door. She scrambled out of bed, leaped over Eddie, and slid down the ladder. Mom was still asleep, her bedroom door shut.

Fin unlocked the door and found Cedar standing on

the porch. Her normally sleek hair was mussed. "Some creature came through town." She held out both hands, fingers out wide. "It left behind big, big tracks. Not like a cougar or a bear—but something else. Mom nearly twisted her ankle falling into one when she went out jogging this morning."

Fin pressed a hand to her forehead. "Maybe it was the thing I saw last night."

"You saw something?"

"I'll tell you everything," said Fin. "But first I need to wake Eddie." She ducked back inside the cottage, picking up one of his sneakers. She squinted at the loft, judging her aim, then tossed it. The shoe wouldn't hit him—hopefully—but the thump would be loud enough to rouse even Eddie.

Sure enough, there came a thud followed by a groan. *"Fin,"* Eddie grumbled in a sleep-hoarse voice. "It's spring break. I'm sleeping in. Nothing is worth getting up before eight."

"There are monster tracks in town," said Fin.

There was a moment of utter silence. Then a scrambling, the whisper rustle of a sleeping bag being pushed aside, and the sound of clothes being pulled on.

"Fin?" came a groggy voice from Mom's bedroom. She poked her head through the door, bleary-eyed. She wore a terrycloth robe belted around her pajamas. "What's going on?"

"Monster tracks," said Cedar. "I wanted to show Fin and Eddie!"

Fin's stomach knotted at the sight of Mom's frown. Fin expected her to tell them all to stay away from the footprints. But Mom heaved a sigh and walked into the kitchen, reaching for the coffeepot. "Wear your heavier coat," said Mom. "It's damp out there."

Fin's jaw dropped.

The corner of Mom's mouth twitched. "If you go into the woods, stay on the trails. And stay in a group, okay? I won't worry as much if you're all together." She leaned down to smooth Fin's hair. "I'm trusting you to be safe, okay?"

Eddie appeared at the top of the loft ladder, dressed and carrying one of his shoes. "We will!"

After Fin changed out of her pajamas, they headed into town. "I think I saw the monster that left the tracks last night," said Fin.

"Why didn't you wake me?" asked Eddie, with a trace of irritation. He liked to be in the middle of the action. And he hated when he was the last to know something.

"I tried," said Fin indignantly. "And you mumbled

something that sounded like 'Mom, no,' and went back to sleep."

Eddie's annoyance crumbled into a rueful grin. "Okay, that sounds like me."

They turned onto Main Street, toward Brewed Awakening. Fin liked Aldermere best in the mornings, when the air was bright and crisp and sunlight made the redwood needles glow. A few cars were parked outside the coffee shop; road trippers would often drive into town for coffee and a restroom. Fin saw license plates from Kansas, Washington, and Arizona. But it wasn't the sight of the cars that made her footsteps falter.

The SNACC film crew sat outside Brewed Awakening. They took up a whole table with their cameras, a laptop, and several cups of coffee. Ana Bell had a bagel in one hand and a phone in the other. Her frown was a familiar one—Fin had seen it on the faces of many tourists when they discovered that Aldermere had no cell service. "Do they know?" asked Fin in a low voice. "About the tracks?"

Cedar frowned thoughtfully. "Not sure. There are some out back. This way." She led them around the building, toward several full trash bins. Cedar gently pushed aside a clump of overgrown ferns.

Fin crouched beside her, and Eddie stood over them both.

There were footprints in the damp earth beside the bins. And they definitely weren't human. The prints were too big, with wide toes and sharpened edges that looked like claws. Fin traced the edge of one with her fingertip.

"Interesting," said Eddie. "Whatever it was, it came right up to the garbage."

"Maybe it was hungry," said Fin. She made a face. "If a shadow can get hungry."

Cedar took a step back. "A shadow?"

"Yeah, that's what I saw last night," said Fin.

"Can shadows leave footprints?" asked Eddie, his brow screwed up in thought.

Cedar wrinkled her nose. "Come on. Let's talk about this away from the garbage." They walked back around to the front of the coffee shop. There was an assortment of tables— two circular metal ones with umbrellas overhead and an old picnic table, the cracks filled in with moss and the wood still damp from morning fog. Fin pulled off her coat and set it on the bench before sitting on it. Eddie plopped himself down, not caring if his seat was wet.

The SNACC crew was at the circular table nearest the front door, out of earshot. Still, Fin glanced at them warily. "Wait a minute," said Cedar. She vanished inside and reappeared with three hot chocolates flavored with cinnamon and chili powder. Warmth unfurled in Fin's stomach after the first sip.

"All right," Fin said. She looked at Eddie expectantly. He *was* the animal expert. "What was it?"

"The footprint looked . . . a little human," said Eddie, after taking a gulp of his hot chocolate. "It's got human-ish toes."

"Maybe if that human hadn't clipped their toenails in a year," said Cedar. "And then *sharpened* them."

"The thing I saw was pretty big," said Fin. "Kind of horselike. If a horse made out of shadows kept confusing itself with an antlerless moose. I didn't get a look at its feet, though. Too dark."

"So we're looking for a shadow horse moose with giant human feet and claws," said Eddie brightly.

Fin shuddered. "Thanks for the nightmares, Eddie."

"Anytime," he replied, smiling.

Cedar's fingers tightened on her cup. "What do you mean 'looking for'?"

Eddie's smile widened. "I mean," he said, "we've got to do our part for the town, right? Can't have these filmmakers finding this creature, whatever it is."

Fin looked past Eddie, toward the SNACC Pack. One of the young men was typing on a laptop while the other went inside the coffee shop, carrying a tray of dirty dishes.

"We don't even know if they're looking for it," said Cedar.

"Of course they're going to look for it," said Eddie. "No one can keep giant footprints in town a secret. If they don't already know, they will soon. And if they don't want to investigate whatever made those footprints, I'll eat this napkin holder."

"You just want to meet the monster," said Fin.

Eddie shrugged, unapologetic. "Course I do."

"And what are we going to do if we find it?" said Cedar. "Chase it out of town?"

"I was thinking something more along the lines of . . . lure it out of town with something tasty. I mean, as long as it isn't carnivorous. I'm not that selfless." Eddie looked thoughtful. "If it's friendly, maybe we could teach it to carry riders. Think how much easier your deliveries would be with a shadow horse, Fin!"

"No," said Fin flatly.

"But . . ." began Eddie.

"My mom won't let me have a pet hamster," said Fin. "And your mom refuses to have any indoor pets since you keep bringing snakes into the house. They won't let us keep a monster in the garage."

Eddie sighed, resigned. "Fine. But I still think we need to

track it down. If it's hiding out behind the film crew's van or something, we can tell one of the adults. Let them handle—" He cut off abruptly, his expression darkening.

Fin looked over her shoulder. Standing only a few steps away was Scott River. He watched them, his brows drawn together and his mouth scrunched to one side.

Cedar held up her hand and waved at him. "Hi, Scott!"

"Edward," River said. A look at Fin. "Edward's cousin." Lastly, toward Cedar. His frown deepened. "Uh, whoever you are."

Cedar exhaled softly.

Once, Fin would have ducked her head and stayed quiet. But now her temper flared on Cedar's behalf. "That was rude," said Fin. "You should apologize."

"It's fine," Cedar said, so quietly that Fin barely heard her.

"It's not," said Fin.

"Whatever." River turned, hands shoved in his pockets, and shuffled into Brewed Awakening.

"Now you understand why I don't like him?" said Eddie. He drained the last of his hot chocolate. "He's a jerk."

"He's upset," said Cedar. "He didn't want to move here, so he's taking it out on us instead of his parents. Maybe that's safer."

Fin gave Cedar a startled glance. Fin hadn't considered *why* River would be rude, but maybe she should have. She and Mom had come to Aldermere because they needed a safe place to stay. It had worked out, but Fin remembered the apprehension when she'd first stepped out of the car and into the unknown. She hadn't belonged, not for a long time.

"We should try to be nice to him," said Fin. Then, after a moment's thought, "At least for the first few weeks. If he's still a jerk after that, Eddie can stick lizards through his bedroom window."

"I wouldn't do that," protested Eddie. "Poor lizards didn't do anything to deserve that."

Fin snorted. The mugs of hot chocolate were empty, and she gathered them up. "I'll bus these, then we can figure out what we're doing next, okay?" She hopped up from the bench, leaving her jacket behind as she hurried around the table toward Brewed Awakening's front door. She had to pass by the SNACC table. It was the closest Fin had come to the film crew, and she found her steps slowing as she looked them over. The cameraman was Black, with curly hair and an assortment of camera lenses strewn before him. Michael, Fin remembered. He was eating a slice of bagel heavy with vegetables, while Ana Bell was flicking through her phone. There was no sign of Ryan Bell, Ana's twin brother.

"... stunt," Ana was saying. "Someone thinks it's hilarious to prank us."

"You really think so?" asked Michael. He picked up a napkin, wiping cream cheese from his fingertips.

"No, Michael," said Ana Bell, her voice heavy with sarcasm. "I think a monster walked through town the very night a cryptozoology team showed up to investigate." She straightened, her gaze sweeping across the neighborhood. "This place looks like it's had better days. They probably need the tourist dollars, and I can't blame them." She picked up a mug. "At least the coffee's decent."

"Did the Wi-Fi work in your room last night?" asked Michael. "Because Ryan spent half the night wandering around our room with his phone in the air, trying to get a signal."

"It worked, but it's slow," said Ana. "Tried to download a podcast and it took twenty minutes. Tell Ryan if he needs to check his email, he can come to my room." Her voice was low and a little hoarse. "Our parents brought us on a family camping trip here when we were kids, you know. Ryan thought he saw Bigfoot, but it turned out to be a weirdly shaped tree."

Michael laughed. "And thus a monster-hunting legend was born."

The corner of Ana's mouth lifted into a smile. "Regardless,

this place has more cryptid sightings per year than even that one forest in Oregon. You know. The one that has the same name as the ice cream."

"Umpqua," said Michael promptly.

Ana drummed her fingers against the metal tabletop. Her nails were a faded green, and she had several rings on each hand. "Even if these footprints are a prank, we still need to follow up. There are some tracks behind the hotel—we should start there."

Fin's stomach lurched in surprise. The shadow monster had come that close to the inn? What if her mom had still been there? She was so intent on that line of thought that it took her a moment to realize the film crew was staring at her. "Hey," said Ana. "Can we help you?"

A flush rose to Fin's cheeks. "Sorry," she mumbled. She hurried toward the coffee shop.

"Such a way with kids, Ana," said Michael, a laugh in his voice.

Inside Brewed Awakening, Fin carefully set the mugs inside a plastic bin marked DIRTY DISHES. The morning rush had calmed; there were only a few people inside—a small family with a toddler, and an older couple. Fin blinked when she saw the last of the SNACC Pack. Ryan was speaking to Mr. Carver.

". . . happy to buy you both dinner and pick your brains," he was saying. He had dark blond hair and the same sharp chin as Ana Bell.

Mr. Carver was smiling, but it looked strained. "That's very kind," he said, "but my wife and I have been out of the business for years now. I don't think we'd be any help."

"You say that," said Ryan, "but you retired to a cryptid hotspot. You have to forgive us for thinking you've still got your foot in the door."

Mr. Carver picked up a damp cloth and began running it over the counter. "You're forgiven. Now, if you'll excuse me . . ." His gaze alighted on Fin. She jumped a little, guilty at being caught eavesdropping a second time in as many minutes. To her relief, Mr. Carver's smile warmed. "Finley. Is Cedar going to your house today? Or are you going to ours?"

"Hey," said Ryan, interrupting. "Could you give me the Wi-Fi password? I saw there's a network here."

Mr. Carver didn't so much as glance at him. "It's for staff use only."

Consternation flashed across Ryan's face; he turned and left the coffee shop.

Fin wrenched her gaze back to Mr. Carver. "I think we're all going hiking," she said, in answer to his original question. "Eddie wants to."

"That's nice. It's a good day for it." Mr. Carver reached down and pulled out a bag filled with stale bread crusts. "For Bower's Creek, if you head that way," he said in a lower voice, so none of the other customers would overhear. Fin nodded her thanks and took the bag.

Locals knew to drop food in the water before touching Bower's Creek—if something dragged the food under, then it wasn't safe to cross.

"And you stay away from those people," said Mr. Carver, with a foreboding glance at the door. "They're going to cause trouble, I know it."

Fin nodded a second time, unsure of how to reply. "See you later, Mr. Carver."

By the time she stepped outside, the film crew was gone. She caught a glimpse of them walking up Main Street toward the inn. They'd be Mom's problem now—and Fin couldn't think of anyone better equipped to handle them. Mom could wear blankness like a mask and be so neutral that they wouldn't get any information out of her.

"What took you so long?" asked Eddie.

"I eavesdropped on the SNACC Pack," said Fin as she approached the picnic table.

Cedar snorted. "SNACC Pack?"

"It's what I've been calling them in my head," said Fin,

with a small shrug. "Easier than Society of Crabby Monster Hunters or whatever their name is."

"And what'd you hear?" Eddie was all but bouncing in place.

"SNACC is going after the tracks," said Fin. "They found some behind the inn, and while Ana thinks they're a prank, they're still going to investigate. And your dad told us to stay away from them," she added to Cedar.

Cedar folded her fingers in her lap, her face all innocence. "Well, he never told us not to find the monster, right?"

"He never said that," Fin agreed. "But SNACC's going to be out there looking too."

Eddie sat up straighter, grinning. "So let's beat them to it."

FIVE

Into the Woods

The first thing they did was return to the tracks.

They chose the ones behind the coffee shop garbage bins, rather than investigate those behind the inn. They'd be more likely to run into the SNACC Pack there, and Mr. Carver's warning was still fresh in Fin's mind. Eddie knelt beside the footprint, his eyes roaming over it as though he were reading a book. He touched the dirt, then rose to his feet.

"This way," he said.

They cut across Redwood Street, past a few vacation rentals and toward one of the northeast hiking trails beyond the town's small magic shop. It sold tarot decks, crystals, herbs, and witches' almanacs. Cedar glanced at the window, where a sign promised a two-for-one sale on dried flowers. "You ever go in there?" she asked.

Fin shook her head. "Once, when I first moved here. She had some pretty bowls. But the owner was . . . well, I don't think she was having a very good day. She was snappy."

Eddie said, "I wonder why."

Fin shrugged. "I don't know. I just never went back."

"Why not?" Eddie seemed befuddled.

"Because," said Fin. She didn't know how to explain that if she went into a shop or store and something went awry, Fin never went back. It was the same reason she'd never bought an iced drink from the corner store near their middle school; she didn't know if she had to pay for the cup first and then get the drink, or get the drink and then pay for it. And if she asked, the clerk might raise his brows in that way that indicated Fin was stupid for not knowing.

Avoidance wasn't a great strategy, she knew. And while she was working on this with her counselor, it didn't make all of Fin's fears vanish overnight.

Eddie was looking at Fin in that way he did sometimes— like he couldn't quite figure her out. But Cedar said, "Yeah, I get it. If you go back, she could remember you. Or worse, she won't remember you and you've built up this huge thing in your brain for nothing."

Fin shot Cedar a grateful, startled glance. She hadn't realized that Cedar would understand.

Eddie shook his head. "I can't decide if you're overthinking or if I never think."

"Both," said Fin.

Eddie snorted and continued to the hiking trail. Together they walked out of town and into the woods.

The dappled sunlight fell through the redwoods overhead, illuminating a thick carpet of sorrel. Tiny purple flowers had sprung up, and moss clung to a few fallen branches. The trail was dirt and redwood needles and the occasional brown sign with information about the forest. Most of the hiking trails went north or south, avoiding the dense eastern forest—the place most rife with magic. The trails were considered safe, kept clear by Aldermere and maintained for the tourists and hikers. Tourists were discouraged from leaving the trails by signs about bears and cougars and notices saying how long it would take for an ambulance to arrive, should someone get hurt.

Eddie pulled ahead, his strides longer than Fin's. Cedar slowed a little, keeping pace with her.

"One of the SNACC Pack was talking to your dad in the coffee shop," said Fin. "I don't think your dad likes him."

Cedar looked at her in surprise. "Which one?"

"Ryan," replied Fin.

"Oh, right." Cedar nodded, her gaze going a little distant. "Ryan Bell. He doesn't do a lot of talking in the episodes, but he's always in charge of research."

"So you've watched some of their stuff?" Fin gently pushed aside an overgrown fern frond, holding it so that Cedar could pass by.

"I watched some yesterday," Cedar admitted.

"Me too," said Fin. "And what'd you think?"

Cedar shrugged. "It's part documentary, part reality show about three twenty-somethings running around the country in their van. Ana Bell's whole thing is that magic isn't real, which is a relief. She was a biology major in college, so she knows how to test DNA and stuff. She's taken a more scientific approach than a lot of the other cryptid hunters."

"If she doesn't believe in magic, why do it?" asked Fin, because this had been bugging her. "It's got to be a lot of work for something she's not into."

"Some people like finding out stuff," said Cedar. "The thrill of the chase and all that. And other people like poking holes in people's beliefs. Maybe Ana Bell wants to know the truth—or maybe she doesn't believe and doesn't want anyone else to, either. Or maybe she couldn't come up with a better idea for a web show."

"How popular are they?" asked Fin. "Compared to other cryptid hunters, I mean."

Cedar huffed. "They have enough subscribers to make a living off it."

"Wow." Fin was genuinely impressed. "I didn't think a person could make a living looking for monsters."

"You can if you're pretty and good at talking to a camera," said Cedar with a wry smile. "They also sell T-shirts and hats and stickers, and some of their episodes are sponsored by some weird energy drink I couldn't pronounce. They're doing well. I mean, they're wearing expensive clothing."

"If it's such a good job, why did your parents stop?" asked Fin. Then she flushed. "Sorry, you don't have to answer that."

"It's fine." Cedar picked up a stick fallen across the trail and tossed it into the undergrowth. "After they had me, my parents did the whole parenting-on-the-road thing for a while. I don't remember—I was too young. But when I was old enough for school, they decided they needed to settle down. They picked Aldermere because they thought they could continue their work. Mom had written a few books on cryptozoology and Dad liked blogging about it, although most of his posts were about the kinds of birds and plants he found in the woods. They wanted to be the ones to find Bigfoot, mostly for conservation reasons. They thought they could save the forests if people knew that rare species were at risk. They were the kind of hippies who chained themselves to trees when they were in college. But after they moved here . . . you know how that worked out."

Fin nodded. Cedar had once told her that Aldermere hadn't welcomed the Carver family, not for many years. Suspicious of outsiders and protective of its secrets, the town hadn't opened up until the Carvers took over Brewed Awakening and gave up looking for monsters. Fin suspected this was why Cedar didn't have many friends. Cedar was pretty and smart and friendly, but it seemed like Fin and Eddie were the only kids she regularly hung out with.

"Is that why your dad didn't like Ryan?" said Fin. "Because . . ." She couldn't quite find the bravery to say her thoughts aloud—that SNACC had accomplished what the Carvers hadn't: making a living out of their cryptozoology.

A knowing smile tugged at Cedar's mouth. "Dad's jealous? Probably a little. But Mom and Dad want to protect Aldermere too." She exhaled, her smile fading.

"You think SNACC could really mess things up," said Fin. It was partly a question and partly not.

Cedar's brows drew together. "I think it's better if we don't give them the chance."

They followed Eddie north, toward the Eel River. He led

them unerringly from one hiking trail to a deer path, finding faint tracks that others would have missed. The creature, whatever it was, didn't want to make its own way through the undergrowth. After about twenty minutes of walking, they stepped out of the tree cover and onto the edge of the gravel road. The old logging road, she realized. They'd circled around Aldermere, coming out at the northwest edge of town.

To her right was a bridge. It was old and wooden, with a heavy chain drawn across it so no one could drive over. NO TRESPASSING, the rusted sign declared. Fin wondered if that bridge could even hold the weight of a car; moss clung to some of the wood and a few of the planks had rotted away.

"The toll bridge," said Eddie.

"We aren't going over it, are we?" asked Cedar. "We're not supposed to."

It was one of the rules of Aldermere: *Don't use the old toll bridge north of town—there is a price, but no one knows what it is.*

In Fin's experience, people in Aldermere didn't always pay with dollars or coins. They paid for magic with memories or something equally precious. And she was wary of taking on a debt that she might not be able to pay.

Eddie squatted down beside one of the monstrous

footprints. "Looks like the creature crossed the road, heading west."

They tromped across the road; it was mostly damp dirt, with a few scattered rocks. There were several potholes that would fill up with one good night of rain. The forest to the west of the road was part of the woods that had been logged, leaving behind stumps and new-growth redwoods that looked like spindly saplings compared to the old growth. Amaryllis bloomed in patches of sunlight.

There was a new hiking trail—this one lined with plaques about the damage logging had done in the old sequoia forests and nature preservation in the future. As they walked past a sign with an illustration of how the forest would have once appeared, Fin paused to look. Cedar stopped beside her, but Eddie kept going. "It's a pretty picture," said Cedar. "I wonder who Mayor Downer hired to draw these."

"Not Aunt Myrtle," said Fin. "She'd—"

But she never finished her sentence.

Something exploded from the undergrowth.

It happened so quickly that Fin barely had time to turn her head before something slammed into her knees. She dropped to the ground, hitting so hard that all the breath was knocked out of her. Redwood needles prickled against her bare palms, and for a few panicked moments, she couldn't inhale. Her lungs would not work.

There was a startled shout that sounded like Eddie. *Oh no—Eddie.* She thought of him up ahead, unprepared for whatever had attacked her. She squeezed her eyes shut, fighting back the panic. She needed to breathe, to just breathe—

Finally she drew in a ragged breath, then another.

"That way!" Eddie was saying.

Pounding footsteps against the ground. And then they faded away.

Fin lay on the dirt path, gazing at tangled blackberry bushes. They needed trimming, some distant part of her noted. This trail's undergrowth was thicker than before, which was probably how that thing had managed to stay hidden long enough to attack her.

A hand, warm and a little sticky with sweat, landed on Fin's wrist. "You okay?" said Cedar. She crouched beside Fin, her dark brown eyes worried.

"What was that?" croaked Fin. "Where's Eddie?"

"It looked like an animal," said Cedar. She rocked back on her heels, resting her elbows on her knees. "I think we scared it—it bolted, ran into you, and darted around Eddie. He went after it."

"We're not supposed to split up." Fin rolled onto her side. Her ribs ached and her breaths were shallow, but at least she could breathe. Cedar held out her hand, her turquoise nail polish glinting in the sunlight. Fin took her hand gratefully, allowing herself to be helped up. She brushed some of the dirt and needles from her pants. "We have to go after him."

They broke into a half jog, half walk. It was difficult to run outright in a forest, even on a trail. The redwood needles could be slippery; rocks and branches could trip a person; there were likely other hikers who might be alerted by the sound.

Fin thought of the creature she had seen the night before—the shadowed equine form that had ghosted through the backyard. Eddie couldn't face that thing alone. Not that Fin thought herself up to facing a shadow monster. But she and Cedar were better than nothing.

They jogged up the trail, winding back and forth as their path took them up a hill. Finally Fin rounded a bend and saw Eddie's familiar form. He stood about five feet from the path, shoulders heaving with exertion.

"It went behind there," said Eddie, pointing at a clump of huckleberry bushes. The greenery was studded with tiny pink flowers, and a bumblebee bobbed merrily from one bloom to the next. It looked peaceful and innocent. Fin didn't trust it for a moment.

"And here we are without a lacrosse stick for defense," she said.

Eddie huffed out a laugh. His eyes were dancing with excitement—the thrill of chasing a new magical creature was what he lived for. Fin's legs were still a bit wobbly, and she would've preferred a few more minutes to catch her breath. But there was no time.

"All right," she said. She glanced around until her gaze alighted on a fallen stick. She picked it up, brushing away some of the old needles. It wasn't much protection, but having something in her hands made her feel braver.

Eddie stepped around the huckleberries, and Fin hurried after. Cedar was close to Fin's side, her hands held out as if to ward off whatever monster was waiting.

It wasn't a shadow monster.

They all gaped at it.

At first glance, it looked a little like an otter. It had the same dark nose and whiskers, with tiny rounded ears tucked into soft fur. It stood on its hind legs, small paws pressed up against itself as if in fear. But it was definitely a creature of magic: tiny mushrooms grew around its neck like a small ruff; its fur was white and brown, striped like a tabby cat;

and most importantly of all—its feet were enormous. They were broad as shovels, tipped with small claws that looked made for digging. Those were the feet that had left the prints throughout town, behind Brewed Awakening and the inn.

And all at once, Fin realized what this creature had to be.

"I told you Bigfoot was real," said Eddie.

SIX
Bread Crumbs and Brie

Fin had known the legend of Bigfoot—or Sasquatch, as he was sometimes called—long before she'd moved to Aldermere.

He was supposed to be a large, apelike creature. One that lived in mountains or forests, who kept to himself save for the occasional late-night documentary. Those films were of people who'd seen or smelled things that didn't belong in Northern California, who glimpsed mangled animals and large rocks hurled toward human settlements. The way those people told it, Bigfoot was a creature who terrorized humans when he bothered to emerge from the shadows.

This small, otterlike creature didn't resemble the legend in the slightest.

For a moment, no one moved. Not even the creature. The *bigfoot*. Fin forced herself to think the word. She had believed in magic for years now. But she never thought she would meet an actual bigfoot.

"That's a bigfoot?" said Fin. "I thought they were . . . bigger."

"That's a baby," said Eddie. "The adults are like fifteen feet tall."

"Aren't they supposed to be scary?" asked Fin, frowning.

The bigfoot made a noise that sounded like *meep*.

"Oh my goodness," cooed Cedar. She squatted down, as if the bigfoot was a stray cat. "Hi there."

"They're not predators," said Eddie. "And they're very shy. At least that's what Nick told me. One wandered into town a few years ago—I never saw her, but some people renting that eastern water tower kept leaving food out."

The bigfoot cowered, but Fin knew better than to let her guard down. Fear only made some creatures—and people— more dangerous.

"If that's a baby," said Cedar, keeping her voice low and soothing, "where are its parents?"

Eddie frowned. "She must have gotten separated from her herd."

"That's what I felt last night, then," Fin said. "The ground was shaking a little—it must have been a bunch of bigfoots moving through the woods."

The bigfoot's ears twitched, moving back and forth as if it was listening to Fin's every word.

"Is this the creature you saw?" said Eddie.

Fin shook her head. "No, definitely not. What I saw was much scarier. And bigger."

"Maybe that shadow creature chased her away from her herd," said Eddie. "She could've been trying to escape it."

Fin thought of the long-legged shadow and shivered. "Yeah. I could see even a bigfoot being afraid of it."

"Hey," Cedar said, voice soft. "It's okay. We're not scary, I promise."

The bigfoot's dark gaze flicked from Eddie to Cedar to Fin, then over its own shoulder. It appeared to yearn for the woods behind it.

"Why isn't it running?" murmured Fin, trying to keep her mouth from moving too much. She didn't want to startle it a second time.

"Maybe it's tired," said Cedar. "Poor thing must have been scared all night, if it got lost."

Fin began to shrug off her coat. Sweat had beaded up behind her T-shirt and she was too warm after their run through the forest. The bag Mr. Carver had given her fell from the coat pocket. It tumbled to the ground, spilling several crusts.

The bigfoot's ears pricked forward. It edged toward the food but wasn't brave enough to venture closer.

Fin didn't have Eddie's affinity for animals, but even she understood. "Are you hungry?" she said. She picked up the bag and tossed one crust toward the bigfoot. The creature scooped it up with those otterlike paws and began devouring it.

"She's starving," said Eddie, clapping a fist into the palm of his other hand. "That's why she came into town and looked around the dumpsters near Brewed Awakening. I bet she poked around the inn's trash too. She's too young to forage for her own food yet. And without her parents, she's desperate."

"She?" asked Fin.

"I think it's a female," said Eddie. "Pretty sure."

"She's adorable," said Cedar. "Look at those whiskers! And her little paws."

The bigfoot finished the crust and began cleaning her face, running her paws over her whiskers and ears the way a rabbit might. Fin softened toward the bigfoot, the last vestiges of fear draining away. This creature wasn't monstrous—she was hungry and scared. If she had been fleeing that shadow,

Fin could understand why the bigfoot had risked coming into town.

The bigfoot lifted her head, her small ears moving back and forth as she listened.

And then Fin heard it—the footsteps. A cracking branch, the rustle of undergrowth.

Adrenaline jolted through her in a hot rush. Fin's gaze jerked around until it landed on the hiking path only a few feet away.

"Someone's coming," Cedar whispered. "What if they see her?"

All of them gazed at the bigfoot for a heartbeat, then Fin tore into the bag of bread. "Come on," she said in a low voice. "Come here . . . uh . . . you." She waggled a crust of bread at the bigfoot.

The creature's head tilted, curious. But she didn't move. Fin gritted her teeth, resisting the urge to give into her frustration. They couldn't risk startling the creature and driving her toward the hiking trail.

Fin tore off a small bit of crust and tossed it into a large clump of ferns. The bigfoot gave Fin a wary, confused look. Then she scurried into the bushes and out of sight.

"Good idea," said Eddie. "Cedar, come here." He took two steps sideways, so he stood between the ferns and the trail. "If we stand here . . . they might not see anything."

"Yeah," said Cedar, and hurried to his side.

Fin walked as quickly and quietly as she could, around the thick ferns to where the bigfoot had found the bread. She was nibbling away at the crust, holding it between her tiny paws and getting crumbs all over her whiskers. Luckily, she didn't mind Fin's presence.

Fin crouched behind the ferns, listening. The only sounds were the soft *click-click* of the bigfoot's teeth and the approaching footsteps. Fin tried to slow her breathing, to make it less audible.

"Morning," came an unfamiliar voice. Fin peered through the bushes and saw a boy and a girl. They were perhaps fourteen or fifteen, wearing sneakers that would be ruined on a muddy trail. Definitely tourists.

"Morning," said Cedar and Eddie in one voice.

"Is this the trail that leads to that big redwood?" said the boy.

"No," said Cedar. "There's a trail across town, going east, and it leads to that big one. I forget what the name is."

"Delilah," said Eddie helpfully. "Big Delilah. She's marked along the trail. Supposed to be almost a thousand years old."

The bigfoot finished her snack and lifted her head,

listening. Fin's heart thudded in her chest. She fumbled another bread crust out of the bag.

The bigfoot's gaze darted toward the tourists, then back to the bread. Fin held her breath, silently hoping that she wouldn't investigate the strangers.

The bigfoot picked up the crust and began eating.

"Thanks," said the girl. There was a rustle, as if she'd elbowed the boy. "I told you it was in the other direction." There was the sound of footsteps against the dirt path, returning the way they had come. Fin didn't move until she couldn't hear them.

She rose from her crouch. At least they were safe. For now.

"That was close," said Cedar. "Is she still . . . ?"

"Eating?" said Fin. "Yup."

They walked around the ferns to see the bigfoot. She regarded them without fear, probably because Fin kept feeding her. Which wasn't a great solution, Fin knew. Wildlife was supposed to be wild. But the magic also had to be kept secret, and this adorable creature with her oversized feet and otter's face didn't seem to understand that.

For a few moments, they all looked at the bigfoot.

"We can't leave her here," said Fin, breaking the silence.

"She could wander into town again—and imagine what the SNACC Pack would do if they saw her."

Concern crossed Cedar's face. "They'd take her away. Probably to a lab or something. She'd never see her parents again." She straightened. "You're right—we can't leave her here."

Eddie grinned. "So much for 'My mom won't let me have a pet.'"

"She's not a pet," protested Fin. "I'm just saying—Nick will know what to do with her. We can take her back to . . . I don't know where."

"What about your cottage?" said Cedar. "Your mom is working today, so it'll be empty. And the bigfoot will be in familiar territory, but not in town. And if we show her it's safe and there's food, she'll probably be fine."

Sure enough, the bigfoot was sniffing in Fin's direction, her eyes on the bag of bread.

"We'll have to lure her all the way to the cottage, then," said Eddie.

Fin pulled out another crust. "I think I know how to do that."

Of all the things Fin had planned for spring break, she hadn't expected to lure a baby bigfoot back to her cottage with a trail of breadcrumbs. It took the better part of an hour—she had to sprinkle the crumbs, wait for the bigfoot to eat them, then step back about fifteen feet and sprinkle more. Luckily, the bigfoot never tired of the stale snack; she kept shuffling after Fin, her big dark eyes on the bag of food. Eddie kept up a steady stream of soothing chatter, trying to get the bigfoot used to the sound of his voice. Cedar followed a few feet behind, quiet and watchful. They kept to the woods, peering warily at the old logging road before hurrying across. That wide expanse of open air and gravel felt dangerous; there was no place to hide. Fin didn't know how they would explain the bigfoot to any tourists who might glimpse her.

Finally the familiar redwoods near Fin's cottage came into view. She heaved a sigh of relief.

"No one's home," she said. "But someone should probably still keep watch near the big house, make sure none of the neighbors come by."

Cedar nodded. "I can do that." She turned and trotted toward the big house.

Fin tossed a few more breadcrumbs onto the porch. The bigfoot shuffled up the steps, picking up each crumb with her deft little paws. Fin carefully unlocked the cottage door and stepped inside, sprinkling a few more crumbs. "Your mom would freak if she knew what you're bringing inside," said Eddie, grinning. He sounded proud of Fin's new bout of rule breaking. Fin wasn't sure if what she was doing was right—but she was pretty sure they didn't have many other options.

"Well, Mom doesn't have to know," she replied. "We'll be out of here long before she's back from work. And we need more food to keep Bigfoot here occupied. I'm out of bread." She crumpled the empty bag and put it into the trash bin.

Luckily, the bigfoot wasn't interested in destroying the cottage. She merely picked up the last of the crumbs and looked around curiously for more. Eddie shut the door behind her, leaning against it. "What else can we feed her?"

Fin opened the fridge. There was an assortment of old greens in the crisper drawer; a plate with the last of the frittata was on the first shelf, along with a plate of Brie cheese with a note that said *For Book Club at Inn Tonight—DO NOT EAT*. The top shelf held a scattering of yogurt containers, a half-empty mustard bottle on its side, and the butter dish. Fin pulled out the frittata and cheese plates, setting them on the floor so she could rummage in the back. Sure enough, she found a few apples. "They're not into meat, right?"

"Yeah, Nick said they aren't carnivores," said Eddie.

Fin rinsed off the apple, then rolled it across the floor.

The creature eyed the fruit curiously, then picked it up in her tiny paws. She turned it over a few times, and again, Fin was reminded of those videos of otters washing their food. Then the bigfoot took a little bite, nibbling at the apple like a rabbit.

"She is cute, isn't she?" said Fin, shutting the fridge.

Eddie looked elated at the sight of a tiny bigfoot eating an apple. "I've always wanted to see one, but this is . . . wow."

Fin turned toward the kitchen window. It was difficult to believe that only last night, she had watched a shadow monster creep across the lawn through this same window. "What do you think separated her from her family?" she asked quietly. "That monster I saw?"

Eddie came up beside her, peering through the window. "Where'd you see it?"

She pointed at the corner of the big house. "It went around there. But it walked across the entire backyard. You didn't see any tracks?"

"Nothing." Eddie scratched idly at the back of his head. "Do we know yet if shadow monsters leave tracks?"

"I'd ask the internet, but the Wi-Fi doesn't reach out here," said Fin, deadpan.

That earned her a snort of laughter. Eddie's expression grew more thoughtful as he considered the backyard. "Maybe

Nick will know what that shadow thing was."

"I hope so." Fin turned to look at the bigfoot and drew in a sharp gasp. "Oh no."

"What?" Eddie's head whipped toward the bigfoot.

The bigfoot sat before the plate that had once held Mom's Brie cheese—the plate that was now *empty*. Fin felt a rush of panic. Mom was going to be mad; she'd put that cheese away specifically for a book club meeting, and it wasn't as though Fin could explain that a bigfoot had eaten it.

The bigfoot in question was cleaning her whiskers in a self-satisfied way. When Fin let out a groan, the bigfoot looked up at her as if to say, *"What?"*

"She ate the Brie," said Fin faintly. "My mom's going to be mad."

"Just say I ate it," said Eddie, with far more grim bravery than Fin could muster. "She can't get mad at me. I'm the favorite nephew."

The bigfoot, oblivious to their conversation, sidled up to the plate of frittata. Fin scooped that up quickly, setting it on the counter. "You're her only nephew. And she can definitely get mad at you," she said. "She just can't ground you."

"And that's what matters," said Eddie. "Once Mom comes back, *she* can ground me. Or maybe your mom will have forgotten about the cheese by then."

The bigfoot meeped. Then she shuffled up to Fin and leaned against her leg, gazing up with big, warm eyes.

Fin hesitated, then patted the bigfoot on the head. The bigfoot meeped again and closed her eyes contentedly.

It was adorable.

"She likes you," said Eddie.

"I fed her." Fin continued the gentle patting. "She's probably just happy to be full. Like how that stray cat moved himself into the Ack when Mr. Hardin fed him." She looked at Eddie, another squirm of nerves going through her. "She can't stay here. Not forever. Just until we find her family or pack or . . . whatever."

"Are you going to tell your mom?" asked Eddie.

Fin let out a startled laugh. "Definitely not. I mean— she's gotten better about the magic stuff since the tea shop incident. But I don't think she'll be excited about keeping a bigfoot in my loft."

"We'll need a code word then." Eddie's brow furrowed. "So we can talk about her around other people. 'Bigfoot' would be kinda obvious."

The bigfoot's eyes were slipping closed; she seemed tired after the walk to the cottage and her meal of cheese. Fin's gaze returned to the empty plate.

"Brie," she said. "We can call her Brie."

SEVEN

The Care and Feeding of Monsters

Fin knew only a little about magic. Magic was wild and strange and it thrived in a seven-mile radius around Aldermere. Magic could be kept alive within a person or animal for a time, but only if that person visited Aldermere again and again. The magic was what kept some of Aldermere's residents bound to the town. Some loved it, some feared it.

The rules of Aldermere had been cobbled together by people who had seen and understood the town's quirks. Those who had noticed that certain knives were more likely to cut a person and that doors could transport you across town if they weren't labeled. But while locals accepted the magic, few understood how it worked.

Nick was one of those few.

Fin traipsed west toward Highway 101 and Nick's cabin. Eddie had eagerly volunteered to keep an eye on Brie the bigfoot while Cedar ran off to find some replacement cheese and Fin went to Nick for help. Nick had once relocated a bigfoot. If anyone knew what to do about Brie, it would be Nick.

Nick's log cabin had a small porch and a rocking chair. Two tin men made of old cans hung from the eaves. Fin knocked at the door and waited; she wondered if maybe she should check at the gas station first. Then she heard the sound of footsteps and a lock being unlatched. Nick pulled the door open. He wore old jeans, a long-sleeved black shirt, and a guarded expression. But when he saw Fin, he relaxed.

"Ms. Barnes," he said. "What can I do for you?"

Fin hesitated. She glanced over her shoulder; a car was winding its way up Main Street and a few tourists were looking at an informational sign thirty feet away. Nick followed her gaze.

"You want to come inside?" he said. "I was making lunch."

Fin nodded. "Thanks."

Nick's cabin was small but clean and organized. He led Fin into the tiny dining room, where a raven was napping on the back of a chair. "Aletheia," said Nick. "We've got company."

The raven came awake with a start. She glanced around the room, then croaked in greeting when she saw Fin. Emboldened by her last few months of interactions with Morri, Fin stepped forward and extended her fingers to the raven. Aletheia cocked her head, then nibbled gently at Fin's fingernails. Fin scratched at the soft feathers near Aletheia's beak. The raven closed her eyes and leaned in to the touch.

"You're good with her," said Nick. His kitchen was an alcove off the dining room; the small bit of counter was crowded with what looked like the makings of a salad. Nick picked up a knife and a carrot and began slicing.

Fin flushed at the compliment. "I've learned a little about ravens," she said. A breath, a hesitation, then she added, "But I need to know more about a different animal."

Nick dropped the bits of carrot into a bowl brimming with greens. "And what would that be?"

There was no way to dance around the subject—and besides, Nick had proven himself a dedicated protector of Aldermere. He wouldn't tell anyone. "A bigfoot. A real one."

Nick set down the knife. He leaned with his elbows on

the counter, raising both eyebrows at Fin. "That so? This for your own curiosity or . . ."

"I have a baby one asleep in my cottage," she said. "We found her near one of the northwest hiking trails. She left tracks all through town last night, and the SNACC Pack—"

"The what?"

"The film crew," she explained. "We're calling them the SNACC Pack. It's shorter than the Society of North American Cagey Creatures—or something like that."

For a brief moment, Nick's face broke into a full grin. "I see."

"We think she's too young to find food for herself," said Fin. "She ate a bunch of bread crusts and a plate of Brie, but I don't know what to do with her. Eddie said you relocated one a few years back, before I moved to Aldermere. We can't let SNACC find her, right? I was hoping you'd help."

Nick ran a clean cloth across the knife's edge, then hung the blade from a magnetic strip above his sink. Coming around the counter, he sat in one of the two dining room chairs. Fin took this as a cue and sat in the other—the one that Aletheia was perched on. The raven immediately began trying to groom Fin's unruly brown hair.

"Ah," he said quietly. "And is that all?"

There was something in the way he said it that made Fin

think he knew exactly what she had glimpsed last night.

"I saw a shadow monster too," she said. "Big, like a horse or a moose. It didn't look like one of the regular deer shadows, because it didn't have antlers or human arms. I think that's what separated the baby bigfoot from her parents."

Nick nodded, his long fingers tapping thoughtfully on the tabletop. "Why didn't you go to your aunt?"

"She's in Mendocino at an art show," said Fin. "And I'd ask my mom, but . . ." She let the sentence trail off into a shrug.

"She's not comfortable with magic," said Nick. "Understandable, considering her past with it."

"Do you know what it was?" asked Fin. "That shadow thing?"

Nick did not answer right away. His gaze went distant, as if drawn into memories, and his fingers stroked the faint scar across his mouth. "The first thing you have to know is that a shadow is cast. It does not manifest on its own."

Fin sat up straighter. "But there was nothing—"

"That you saw," said Nick. "But for a shadow to exist, even one made of magic, it must have a source. Perhaps the source was not nearby or not visible to your eyes. But that creature did not exist of its own accord."

Fin remembered the long-legged grace of the monster.

"I don't think I want to meet whatever could cast a shadow like that."

"Maybe, maybe not," said Nick evenly. Fin had the impression that he wanted her to draw her own conclusions. "But either way, I'd say the bigfoot is the—ah, bigger problem at the moment." He settled his hands on the table, clasping his fingers. "You have to be the one to deal with it."

A tendril of panic rose in Fin's chest, threatening to curl around her ribs the way a snake squeezed its prey. She tried to breathe more evenly, to feel the fear and let it pass. That was what her counselor always said: to let herself feel what she needed to feel, rather than tamping it down. It worked . . . sort of.

But still, she didn't *want* to be responsible for the bigfoot. She wanted to cede the dilemma to someone older, more capable. She wanted Nick to fix things.

"Why?" she said.

Nick considered her before answering. He had the keen and intense gaze of an old guard dog, and it was always a little disconcerting to be the object of his attention. "Haven't you ever wondered why the legend of Bigfoot has never been confirmed?"

Fin shrugged. "Because all the pictures look like a guy in a monkey suit?"

"You're not wrong," replied Nick, his eyes warm with humor. "You know they filmed parts of the third Star Wars film in Northern California. The actor who played the Wookie was warned not to wander off the set while in his costume, for fear that bigfoot hunters would shoot him."

Fin let out a small laugh. "Well, Brie doesn't look like a Wookie, so maybe she's safe."

"Brie?"

"It's what we've started calling her," said Fin.

"And how does she act around you?" he said.

Fin considered the last few hours. "She was scared at first. I think we startled her. But after we fed her, she seemed to trust us." A thought occurred to her. "She's . . . friendly. Not scared of humans. If all of them are like that, then why haven't they been discovered yet?"

"Because," said Nick, "she's a juvenile. And so are you. Bigfoots can smell how old humans are—they're a bit like wolves in that respect. They can smell everything about you from your age to your mood to whether you're carrying something tasty. A bigfoot won't come near a conscious adult human. It's a defensive technique. If I tried to go near this Brie, she would start making a high-pitched noise meant to summon every bigfoot in the area."

Fin's stomach clenched. "That sounds bad."

"You're right," said Nick. "They're peaceful, but they are also very protective of their young. There are so few of them left, they cannot afford to lose any offspring." He gave Fin a meaningful look. "You're going to have to be very careful about this. You have a creature that is clearly magical, within a stone's throw of the town and a film crew looking for magic. Were this Brie to panic and start summoning every bigfoot nearby, I'm certain even our best attempts couldn't stop the film crew from seeing them."

"And that shadow monster is still out there." Fin's thumb absentmindedly ran over a dent in her chair. "So what do you think we should do?"

"I think," said Nick, "that you should return her to the herd. I can give you some possible locations. Migratory paths. They aren't like most of our other cryptids—they have no need to stay within the boundaries of the magic around Aldermere. But I doubt the herd will move on if one of their young is still missing."

Fin squinted at him. "If bigfoots never come near adults, then how did you relocate one?"

"I left a trail of food," he said drily, "and remained upwind." He let out a breath. "Well, I suppose you'll want to know what to feed the creature. Bread and apples are fine, but you might want to keep her away from cheese. They're like dogs in that respect. I suspect that your cottage might be rather . . . strong smelling in the hours to come."

Fin mentally added bigfoot farts to the list of things she hadn't ever expected to consider.

"Find the herd," said Nick. "Return her to them. And do so quietly."

When she walked out of Nick's cabin, Fin was armed with a handwritten list of places to search, the correct foods to give to a juvenile bigfoot, and a word of warning. Nick held the door open for her. The day had passed quickly; mid-afternoon sunlight stippled the gravel at the edge of the road and heat rose gently from the pavement.

"Be careful, Ms. Barnes," said Nick.

Fin turned to look over her shoulder to where Nick stood framed in his doorway, Aletheia on his shoulder. "Monsters in the forest are one thing—but monsters in town are something else altogether."

Then he added, "And the only way to avoid shadows is to go somewhere too light or dark to cast them."

Fin loved the redwoods.

She loved the red-brown bark, the way the fallen needles carpeted the ground like snow, their smell of sun-warmed spice, and the way the trees cast the world into silence and dappled shadows. But now Fin found herself watching those shadows warily. She kept well away from them as she walked home. Exhaustion was beginning to weigh on her; after a night of broken sleep and a day of tromping through the forest, she wanted a few minutes to rest.

She rounded the corner and halted in her tracks. A man was on the roof of the big house.

He had dark hair that curled out from beneath a red beanie hat, and his beard was neatly trimmed. *Frank,* Fin realized with some relief. He was around Aunt Myrtle's age. With his flannel shirt rolled up around his elbows and a hoodie tied at his waist, all he lacked was an ax to complete his lumberjack image.

Frank waved down at her. "Hey."

"Hey." Fin put up her own hand in an obligatory greeting. "What are you doing?"

"Your aunt asked if I would look over her roof," said Frank. "Since I worked on the cottage last fall." He thumped one foot against the black shingles. "Still in good condition, though."

Fin didn't know how to answer, so she stayed quiet as Frank walked to the edge of the roof and descended by a metal ladder. He must have brought it, because the only ladder Aunt Myrtle owned was an old wooden one that Fin refused to climb.

Frank walked up to her, swinging his arms a little awkwardly, as though he didn't know what to do with them. He was very tall, and his bare forearms were flecked with a few scars.

"Your mom at work?" asked Frank. The line of his shoulders angled toward the cottage, one foot lifting as if he was going to step in that direction.

Fin couldn't let him go near that cottage. Brie might still be asleep . . . or she might not be. And Nick's warnings were fresh in her mind.

No adults could go near Brie, not without risking discovery and maybe calling every bigfoot in the area. Fin imagined an army of bigfoots coming into Aldermere. Or what had Eddie called them? A herd? Or would it be a pack or—*no*, she decided. A *pandemonium*. It would definitely be a pandemonium of bigfoots.

"Yeah," said Fin, a beat too late to sound natural. "Mom's at the inn. And our roof is fine since you repaired it last fall." She hoped her attempt to keep him away from the cottage wasn't too obvious.

Frank shifted on his feet, rubbing at his knuckles with his other hand. It was a nervous gesture, and that made Fin blink. She didn't know many adults who got nervous talking to kids. "I've got some rhododendrons a gardener friend gave me, and it's too many for my backyard. I thought she might want some."

"Oh," said Fin, surprised. Mom did like flowers—rhododendrons in particular. She wondered if Frank knew or if it was a coincidence. "I think she'd like them. We've got some space beside the cottage that she keeps talking about turning into a small garden."

Frank nodded. "I've got 'em in the back of my truck right now. You could pick out a few."

"Sure," she said.

"All right," said Frank agreeably. He hefted the metal ladder, folding it to a shorter length and then tucking it easily under one arm. Fin trailed in his rather sizable shadow. From the back, she caught a glimpse of the sweatshirt bound around his waist. There was movement in the hood—and then a tiny white ferret peered up at Fin. It blinked once before vanishing back into the hood.

There were times when Fin wondered if anyone truly *normal* lived in Aldermere.

But then again, she'd never been all that normal herself. Maybe that was why she liked it here so much.

Frank's truck was worn but well-kept, with gray paint and a bumper sticker that advertised Aldermere Grocery & Tackle. He carefully slid the ladder into the bed, then reached for several potted plants. The rhododendrons were green and cheerful in their three-gallon pots. Fin's stomach sank. They looked heavy. Frank would probably insist on carrying them to the cottage—and she didn't know any polite way to stop him.

"Here," said Frank, checking one of the handwritten labels. "This one's s'posed to be pink and white. And here's an orange-and-yellow one. And . . . what's your favorite color?"

Fin wracked her brain for an answer. "Uh . . . blue?"

He let out a soft chuckle. "Don't have any blue ones, but here's a purple. Close enough?"

"That sounds great." Fin smiled, but it was a little pinched.

Frank hefted the three rhododendrons out of his truck, setting them down on the edge of the driveway.

"Thanks so much," said Fin, rushing the words. "I'm sure Mom will like them."

Frank smiled—and Fin realized it was the first time she'd ever seen him smile. It softened the edges of his eyes, made his whole face look younger. "Good. Angelina works hard—you both do. Where do you want me to put them?"

Fin took a breath. This was the moment she knew was

coming, but still she braced herself. "I can carry them back to the cottage."

Frank's dark brows twitched in a silent question. His gaze trailed down her arms and she tucked them closer to her sides. She was keenly aware of how skinny her arms looked. She'd never been athletic.

"You sure?" he asked. "I don't mind."

She swallowed, and her throat was too dry. "Yeah," she said. "I've got it."

Fin expected him to brush away her words, to pick up the potted plants and start walking toward the cottage. Not because he was mean or impolite, but because that was what most adults *did*. But to her surprise, Frank nodded. "You tell that cousin of yours if he wants to learn more tracking, he's got to help find the mice that're living in my cupboards. Don't want to put traps out, but I can't have them stealing Molly's food."

"Molly?" said Fin.

Frank reached into the folds of his sweatshirt, pulling out the white ferret. It settled on his shoulder, tiny paws grasping at his collar. "Molly," he said in explanation. "Some tourists abandoned her few years back. Decided I might as well keep her."

"Ah," said Fin, relieved to have an explanation. And

finally a name for the ferret. Things never felt quite real or settled until they had names. "I'm sure Eddie would help. I'll tell him."

Frank gave her another smile, this one a little smaller but no less heartfelt. "Take care of yourself, Fin."

As he was getting back into his truck, Fin reached down to pick up the first of the rhododendrons. It was heavier than it looked; she'd have to haul them one at a time. But still, it was better than Brie being discovered.

With a sigh, Fin hefted the plant into her arms and began half walking, half waddling back home.

Ten minutes later, Cedar returned with a block of sharp cheddar so Mom would have something for her book club. ("It's the best I could find!") Eddie emerged from the cottage with his own discoveries. ("Okay, we are *not* giving her more cheese.") They met on the edge of the forest while Fin relayed all that Nick had told her. She spread out the sheet of paper he'd given her, with the list of places that bigfoots might be. Eddie picked up the paper, his gaze roaming over the list. Fin could see his brain whirling as he considered hiking trails and other paths.

But first they needed a place to stash a bigfoot.

"We can't keep Brie in the cottage," said Fin. "Mom may

not always notice when I do weird things, but she's definitely going to see a bigfoot baby sleeping on her workout shoes."

"How about the garage?" suggested Eddie. "Mom never parks her car in there—it's full of old junk."

Fin considered it. The garage would be an ideal place to keep Brie: it was secure and the odds of anyone going in there were pretty low. But then she shook her head. "Too close to the street," she said. "If anyone walks by . . . well. I think Brie only ventured into town at two in the morning because all the adults were asleep. If an adult wandered too close in the daytime, she could start panicking. And Nick said that her cries could call every bigfoot nearby."

"This sounds like the start of a bad horror film," said Cedar with a wicked grin. *"Bigfoot Invades, Part Two!"*

"Because Part One was Brie rummaging around in people's garbage cans," said Eddie.

"Exactly," replied Cedar.

Fin rolled her eyes toward the sky. "I'm glad you two are having fun."

"You know I deal with stress by making bad jokes," said Eddie. He touched a finger to his chin, tapping thoughtfully. "I might have an idea, though. In the garage—"

"I just said . . ." began Fin.

"—I have a tent," said Eddie, holding up his hand for

silence. "Mom and I sometimes go camping down south. We haven't used it for a while. So it'll probably be really dusty and full of spiders. But if we set it up within the boundaries of the forest, behind the cottage, no one will come across it. We're not close to any hiking trails. And your mom doesn't go into the forest, so she wouldn't see it."

Fin closed her mouth. She considered for a moment, then said, "That's actually not a bad idea."

"I do have them sometimes," said Eddie.

"Will a tent hold her?" asked Cedar.

"We're not keeping her hostage." Eddie shrugged a little. "She hasn't been trying to climb the cottage walls. I think if we keep her company and feed her, she'll be fine in a tent."

"And we'll keep those flap things closed," said Fin.

"Flap things," repeated Eddie, grinning.

Fin snorted. "I'm not a camping person. I don't even know how to set up a tent."

"Good thing you've got me," said Eddie.

It was true. Fin was very grateful her cousin was outdoorsy.

Eddie went to retrieve the tent from the garage while Fin and Cedar returned to the cottage. Fin carefully opened the door. To her relief, Brie was curled up amid a pile of shoes, her eyes closed. Cedar quietly shut the door, and she and Fin spent a few minutes gazing at the bigfoot.

Brie was truly a creature of magic. She looked as though she had climbed out of a storybook, mushroom ruff and all, with her big nose and cute little paws. Her face moved as she dreamed, her whiskers twitching. Fin wondered what a bigfoot would dream of. Humans? Other magical creatures? Or giant plates of brie cheese?

Cedar put the bag with the cheddar cheese in the fridge. Fin saw she'd written on the side *Eddie ate brie. Sorry!* as an explanation. "It was the only good cheese I could find at the Ack," said Cedar, quietly shutting the fridge.

"You didn't have to do that, but thanks," said Fin gratefully.

Cedar gave her a small smile. "I didn't mind." Her gaze fell onto Brie the bigfoot, and her expression became more contemplative. "You sure your mom won't wander into the woods and scare her?"

Fin shook her head. "Mom's not a fan of the woods. She only goes on hiking trails with other people, and usually when there's no way to get out of it."

"Should we tell her anyways? Or someone else?" said Cedar.

Fin had been considering that very question. "No," she said. "Not yet, at least. Mom wouldn't be happy with us messing around with normal wildlife—I can't imagine her reaction to finding a bigfoot behind the cottage." She hesitated, chewing on her lower lip. "Things are good and I kind of . . ."

"Don't want to screw that up?" said Cedar. Her tone was understanding. "Yeah, I get that."

"Aunt Myrtle would probably help, but she'd tell Mom. As part of the mom pact or something." Fin glanced at the window, toward the big house. "So it's just us."

There was a moment of quiet, and Fin realized her own mistake. She'd never once considered telling Cedar's parents. They had dedicated a good chunk of their lives to finding the very creature now napping on a pile of shoes. She felt a little rush of shame for not remembering.

Fin scrambled to say, "I mean, unless you want to go to your mom and dad."

Cedar wasn't looking at Fin; her gaze was unfocused, in the direction of the eastern forest. Then she gave a slight shake of her head. "I thought about it. But . . . I don't think so. Mom and Dad would want to help. But I'm not sure they'd be willing to keep that help at a distance. So for now I think we should keep it to the three of us."

"Okay," said Fin.

There came a thud from the porch. Both Cedar and Fin

jumped, and Fin's heartbeat quickened. Surely Mom wasn't home yet, was she?

Brie awoke with a small snort. She sat up blearily, blinking her large eyes. To Fin's relief, Brie wasn't scared.

The front door opened and Eddie poked his head inside. "Got the tents. Let's go set them up."

"What do you mean, tents?" Fin put a little emphasis on the plural.

Eddie grinned—and it was a grin that had Fin's stomach in knots. It was a grin that meant they'd be getting into all sorts of trouble.

"Well, we can't leave her out there all by herself, can we?" he said. "We've got two tents. Tonight, we're camping."

EIGHT
Fair and Unfair

Ever since Mom and Fin moved to Aldermere, Mom had worked at the Aldermere Inn.

The inn had existed for nearly as long as Aldermere, but it was only a decade ago that it was purchased by some rich people in San Francisco and renovated into something resembling a modern hotel. It was the biggest business in Aldermere, employing around fifteen people. The building stood at the easternmost edge of town, where Main Street ended. Fin had spent a lot of time there, coming to know the inn nearly as well as her own cottage.

Mom had started at the front desk and worked her way up to assistant manager. Even if it was hard work and required long hours, Fin knew her mom liked it. Angelina Barnes had never stayed in one place long enough to be promoted to a management position before—and she took pride in that.

Fin walked up to the inn with mingled warmth and apprehension. She wasn't here to spend time with Mom. She was here on a mission: Operation Get Mom to Agree to the Kids Camping in the Woods Without Supervision.

"Hi there, how can I help you?" said the woman behind the counter brightly, even before Fin had fully stepped inside. Jo was full-figured and pretty and wore a lot of vintage clothes. She was Bellhop Ben's replacement, and while Fin didn't know her well, she was nice enough.

"Hey, Jo," said Fin.

"Oh, hey, Fin." Once she realized Fin wasn't a customer, Jo's chipper demeanor relaxed and her voice lowered. "You looking for your mom? Or do you have deliveries?"

"Mom," said Fin. "You know where she is?"

"Check the eastern storage closet," said Jo. "The Wi-Fi router's all . . ." She made a buzzing noise, like a robot submerged underwater. "And some of the guests are complaining. I tried fixing it, but unplugging it and plugging it in again didn't help. Maybe you can do it—they say kids are better with tech these days."

"I think kids actually need to spend time around technology to be good with it," said Fin drily. "I don't even own a cell phone."

Jo laughed, but before she could reply, the desk phone rang. She picked it up and gave Fin a nod of farewell. "Hi! Yes, yes, I know. We need a replacement for Mr. Madeira tonight, he called in sick. I was wondering if—"

Fin winced. Mr. Madeira had been calling in sick more often, and Fin knew the reason. His wife suffered from dementia, and rumor had it she'd been getting worse. When the magical tea shop had been in town, Mr. Madeira had used it, trading a few of his own memories so his wife could keep hers. Now he had to rely on conventional medicine.

Fin wound her way through the hallways, past the kitchen, the dining room, and Mom's office, until she finally reached a storage closet. The door was open, but even so, Fin checked the metal label attached to the frame: STORAGE CLOSET. It was second nature to check doors before walking through them. And after accidentally transporting herself into a water tower six months ago, Fin had been doubly cautious.

Mom was on her knees, rummaging around on the first shelf. Wires spilled around her arms, and her normally sleek hair was frizzy. The large wireless router was on its side, its lights blinking steadily.

"Hey," said Fin. "Having internet problems?"

Mom leaned back on her heels. "Is it that obvious?"

"Jo told me," admitted Fin.

"It wouldn't matter that much normally," said Mom. She rose, wiping her arm across her sweaty forehead. "Sometimes guests even like it when the internet goes out, because it makes them feel like they're out in the wilderness. But the film crew was very insistent about needing an internet connection."

Fin took a step back, glancing up and down the hallway. There were guest rooms on either side, but no one could hear them. "Are they here?"

"No idea," said Mom. She closed her eyes for a moment, as if gathering her frayed patience. Then she said, "What can I do for you, sweetheart?"

Fin smiled, a little sheepish. "How'd you know I came to ask for something?"

"Because you're doing that thing where you twist your fingers around," said Mom, with a knowing smile.

Fin dropped her hands to her sides. "Two things. First, Frank dropped off some flowers for you."

Mom blinked in surprise. "He did?"

"Not cut flowers," said Fin. "But these big potted rhododendrons. I hauled them to the cottage."

Mom smiled, her gaze shunting away from Fin's. "Well, that was nice of him. I'll have to send over cookies next time Mr. Madeira makes them." Mom was a decent cook, but it was common knowledge she couldn't bake. "And what was the other thing?"

Fin hesitated. "Can Cedar sleep over for a night or two?"

Mom arched her brows. It was the first time that Fin had ever asked for a friend to stay the night; only she and Eddie ever had sleepovers, and Fin wasn't sure he counted since he was family.

"You are getting to that age, aren't you?" Mom murmured, as if to herself. Then, more loudly, "Has she asked her parents?"

"She's doing that right now," said Fin. "But she thinks they'll say yes."

Mom crossed her arms, her face thoughtful. She hadn't said yes, but she also hadn't said no. Fin knew Mom had to be worried about being responsible for another kid, especially with Aunt Myrtle gone. "I don't think there's enough room in the loft for three of you," said Mom. "And I don't want you all in the big house alone."

Fin nodded. "We thought of that. Eddie wants to camp

outside. He's got two tents that he and Aunt Myrtle have used before. He can take one, and Cedar and I get the other. There's a little spot out behind the cottage that would work."

Mom's mouth twitched. "You. Want to sleep outside." Laughter simmered beneath every word.

Fin shrugged, trying to appear nonchalant. "I mean, how bad can it be?"

"You still make me and Eddie carry out the big carpenter ants that get into the cottage," said Mom. "Forgive me for thinking you're not the camping type."

"Well, that's only a problem if carpenter ants invade our tent." But Fin was smiling, because she knew she'd won.

"As long as Cedar's parents agree," said Mom. "And I'll be checking, because after this Wi-Fi fiasco, I'm going to need a latte."

Fin nodded eagerly. "Thank you, thank you, thank you!" She rushed forward and gave Mom a quick squeeze around her middle.

Mom hugged her back, dropping a kiss against Fin's hair. "I'm glad you and Cedar have become friends. She seems like a nice girl."

"She is." Fin took a step back, then added in a rush, "Oh, by the way. Eddie accidentally ate your book club Brie. But we replaced it with some cheddar. Thanks for the sleepover—bye!" And she turned and hurried away before her words could sink in.

Fin left the inn through a side door, skirting around a few guests in the parking lot. The SNACC van was parked in the same spot, sunlight gleaming across the painted logo. Wherever Ana Bell and the rest of the SNACC Pack had gone, they didn't need a car. Which meant they were probably exploring the forest.

It didn't matter, Fin told herself. Brie was safe and secret—for now, anyway.

It was a weekend, which meant the Foragers' Market occupied most of Redwood Street. Fin veered right, turning down the bustling street. She liked the fair, even if she rarely bought anything. Many of the stores and shops of Aldermere set up little carts or stands: Brewed Awakening sold cups of coffee and tisanes; the gift shop had postcards, plush toy monsters, and tiny redwood carvings of Bigfoot; the bakery sold loaves of fresh sourdough and rye; and the small bookshop would bring out an assortment of bestsellers. Even Aunt Myrtle would sometimes bring a folding card table and give tarot readings to tourists.

But the rest of the market consisted of foragers, people who lived off the grid and came into town to sell what they found or grew in the forest. Fin always liked to browse their wares because they changed from week to week, season to season. The foods were a wild assortment—there were balls of cheese rolled in black sage, peppercorns, and sea salt; a man who smoked fish with California juniper; twine bundles of dried herbs hanging upside down and swaying in the breeze; jams of olallieberries, huckleberries, and blackberries; sunlight glowing through home-bottled sodas flavored with pine needles, lemon, and honey. There was a couple who always had a stall full of home-sewn crafts with everything from reusable tote bags to knitted hats, and an older woman sold pressed flowers and vintage jewelry.

Fin walked slowly down the row of tables and booths, letting her gaze dart back and forth as she took everything in. It was the best kind of afternoon for the market: sunlight warming the air and a gentle breeze wafting through the trees.

Fin slowed by the vendor with the jewelry, her eye drawn by a vintage locket swinging from a small wooden tree. The older woman was chatting with another vendor, and Fin took a moment to study the locket. It was a simple oval, inlaid with silver meant to look like lace. It was beautiful— and forty-five dollars, which meant Fin would never be able to afford it. And besides, Fin's style tended toward the more practical; her favorite coat was old army surplus and she wore mostly boots, jeans, and T-shirts. This locket was far too delicate for her. But part of her still longed for it.

"What is all this stuff?" said a familiar voice.

Fin looked up and found River standing a few feet away. He wore the wrong clothes for Aldermere: flimsy sneakers and a sweater that would snag on briars. His glasses had slipped down his nose, and he shoved them back into place with an irritated little gesture.

"What?" said Fin.

"I mean," said River, "what type of farmers' market is this?"

"It's not a farmers' market," said Fin. "It's the Foragers' Market."

River looked at her, blond brows arched. "What's the difference?"

"'Forager' has a few different letters than 'farmer.'" Perhaps Fin should have been nicer to him, but River's tone made her hackles rise. He spoke of the market as if there was something wrong with it.

She expected him to snarl in reply, but to her surprise a smile flitted across his face. It was gone so quickly she couldn't be sure she'd actually seen it. "True," he said. He shoved his hands even farther into his pockets. "This a regular thing?"

"Every weekend," she said. "Except in the off-season."

A few tourists ambled by, their arms laden with tote bags. One bag brimmed with freshly picked miner's lettuce and another sagged under the weight of a wooden garden gnome. River watched them pass. "It's . . . different."

"It's Aldermere," said Fin simply.

River mulled that over. "Why's this town so weird?"

Fin shrugged. He wasn't a local, and he'd said his family wasn't staying. He didn't need to know why Aldermere labeled every doorway, why Bower's Creek had clearly marked bridges for tourists to use, or why no one sold matches in town. He didn't believe in magic, which meant he couldn't be trusted to protect it.

"If you hate it so much, why'd you move here?" asked Fin. From what she knew of him, River had lived north of there, in the same town as their school. It wasn't a big town, but it looked like a metropolis compared to Aldermere.

A muscle flickered in River's jaw. "Like I had a choice. We lost our house. Owners wanted to turn it into a vacation rental. There weren't any other places in town we could afford, so my parents expanded the search to include . . . this." He pulled one hand out of his pocket to gesture at Aldermere. "Now I'm going to have to take a bus to school, live in the middle of nowhere, and I can't even call my friends because cell phones don't work and our landline won't be set up for another week." He seemed to deflate, all of his usual arrogance gone—and Fin felt a swell of empathy for him.

"We have a landline," she said. "At my house, I mean. If you need to call someone."

River looked at her sharply. "I didn't ask for your help."

"I know, but—" Fin stumbled over an explanation. She'd only been trying to be nice, but she'd said the wrong thing.

"I'm going to find a way out of here," said River. "I'll find a place for us to live that isn't this hick town full of people who won't talk to my family, and its weird farmers' market, and Edward with his snakes and insects." He brushed past her and she had to take a step back, bumping into the table. All the jewelry jumped, some rings scattering and the locket swinging wildly on its chain.

Fin watched River's back as he strode away, his shoulders hunched.

"Rude," she said, realizing it was the third time she'd uttered that word around River. It was the only offensive thing she could say aloud. She reached down and began picking up the rings, setting them back in their display.

The woman said, "Oh, that's sweet of you, but you don't need to do that." She swooped in, picking up a bracelet that had been knocked askew.

"I don't mind," said Fin. She finished putting the last ring back.

"Were you looking for something in particular?" asked the older woman.

"No, thanks. Just looking." Fin's gaze fell on the rows of old rings. "Your stuff is really pretty. Where do you get it?"

"I find it," said the woman. She wore a flannel shirt and high-waisted jeans. Her hair was pinned up, a few gray strands falling around her face. "Out in the old ghost towns." She smiled. "There were quite a few logging camps back in the day. Many aren't accessible by public roads anymore. But I go around and look through them, see what I can find. You like that locket?"

"Yeah." Fin glanced at the silver locket again. "Where'd it come from?"

"A town farther east," said the woman. "I forget what it's called."

Fin went still. "Redfern?"

"That's the one." The woman snapped her fingers. "You know it?"

"My grandparents were from there," said Fin. "Before they moved to Aldermere."

The woman smiled at her. "You've got roots here."

Fin had never thought about it like that. She liked the

sound of it—as though her family tree was planted someplace safe. "Have a good afternoon," she said, and gave the woman a small wave as she walked away. In the bustle of the fair, it was easy to outpace the memory of River's irritated words. Once, she would have fretted over them, wondering what she had done wrong. But now she knew that his anger had more to do with him than with her.

And besides, Fin had other things to worry about.

"Well," said Fin, "Mom was right. I am not a camping person."

She and Cedar sat on a fallen log. Dry rot had softened the wood to the texture of crumbled stale bread, but it was still sturdy enough as a makeshift bench. The small clearing was only a two-minute walk to the cottage, but the trees hid the tents from view. The needle-carpeted forest floor was springy to the touch and would make a comfortable place to sleep. Setting up the tents had taken them the better part of an hour, involving a lot of fumbling and Eddie squinting at the paper instructions.

"The tents look fine," said Cedar. She was nursing a place on her arm where one of the poles had sprung back and knocked into her. "But I think next time I go camping, I'm going to be a lot nicer to my parents for doing all the work. It's not as easy as it looks."

The two tents were blue and small, set about five feet away from each other. Cedar had come with her parents' permission, a sleeping bag, a backpack with some extra clothes, a toothbrush, and a battery-powered camping lantern.

"There's also a bunch of stale pastries in my bag," said Cedar.

Eddie looked up. He was playing with Brie, waving a small fern frond at her the way a person might toy with a cat. Brie kept reaching for it, using her tiny front paws to try and grab the greenery. "We'll have to hang the food from the trees," he said. "Otherwise bears might show up. Or worse, raccoons."

"You don't think animals will smell her?" said Fin, with a glance at Brie. "I don't think even a bear would mess with a bigfoot."

Brie made a leap for the fern frond and fell onto her backside. She looked puzzled for a moment, then she sneezed.

"Behold the fierce Sasquatch," said Eddie wryly.

"I think Fin's right." Cedar leaned forward, elbows resting on her knees. "The adult bigfoots would be big enough to scare off most predators. Probably all predators. So the smell of even a baby might warn off bears or cougars. They'll think her parents are nearby."

"If only." Fin heaved a sigh. It was too late in the afternoon to go searching for the bigfoot herd. They'd have to venture out in the morning. "One of us is going to have to stay here with her while the others go hiking."

"What are we going to do?" asked Eddie, waving the fern frond again. Brie watched it sway back and forth, her dark eyes intent. "Draw straws?"

"I can stay with her," said Cedar. "I'm not scared of her. Or bears. And besides, you know the trails best and Nick gave this whole mission to Fin."

Fin made a face. "Don't put me in charge of this. Don't put me in charge of anything, please."

"Why not?" said Cedar. "You saved the town once already."

Fin fluttered her hands in the air as if she could ward off the praise. "That was—mostly an accident."

"Still," said Cedar. "You did. And Nick trusts you with this."

"Only because I'm the one who went to talk to him," protested Fin. "If Eddie had gone, he'd be in charge."

"I don't mind being in charge," said Eddie earnestly.

"Which is exactly why you're not," said Cedar. "We need someone who thinks things through, and no offense, Eddie, but I once watched you run right into an anthill and keep going."

Eddie considered, his hands gone still. Brie took the opportunity to seize the fern and begin gnawing on it. She made a face, spat out the frond, and looked at Eddie with a certain amount of betrayal. "Okay, you may have a point," said Eddie. "Fin's in charge. But I probably have the best chance of finding the bigfoot herd, so it should be the two of us trying to find them. If you're really okay with staying behind tomorrow."

"I am." Cedar gestured toward the tents. "I told my parents I was staying here for a few days, and they were fine with it. I think they're glad I'm hanging out with other kids my age."

"And what if we don't find the bigfoot herd?" asked Fin. "What if we find the thing I saw last night? That shadow-horse creature?"

Cedar didn't answer, her gaze falling to the ground. Eddie considered for a few seconds before saying, "Well. We'll go prepared."

"With your lacrosse stick?" said Fin.

Eddie grinned. He reached into the nearest tent and came up with a flashlight. He clicked it on—which would have been more dramatic if it hadn't been daylight, Fin thought. She could barely see the glint of the flashlight's illumination.

"You're going to fight off a shadow with a flashlight," said Fin.

"It's not the worst idea I've ever had, admit it," said Eddie.

Fin gave him a flat look. "That's not saying much."

NINE

Nighttime Visitors

Long after night fell, Fin could not sleep.

It was strange trying to fall asleep outdoors. The sounds of the forest were all around her—the whisper of an evening breeze through the trees, a flap of raven wings, the rustle of Cedar's sleeping bag, and the croak of distant frogs. Eddie didn't mind staying in the same tent as a bigfoot baby, and he fell asleep quickly. So Fin listened to the forest.

Then all went quiet.

The stillness and darkness of a forest could be impenetrable. There was no light at all; the thick tree boughs held moonlight at bay, and the needle-carpeted ground muffled sound.

Fin lay in her sleeping bag and listened to the cadence of Cedar's breaths. The other girl was curled up on her side. Fin wished she could do the same, but her mind was overfull. She kept reaching for the flashlight beside her sleeping bag; she wanted to make sure it was still there.

It wasn't the thought of Brie that kept her awake. The bigfoot was definitely asleep. Fin knew that because it turned out that bigfoots *snored*. There was a soft, rhythmic squeaking sound that came from the other tent.

But Brie wasn't the only monster in the forest.

Had it only been one day since Fin had seen the shadow?

Lying in the dark, it was impossible not to think of the way the creature had moved—as slippery and dark as spilled ink. Such a creature might not be deterred by a tent. The walls around her felt flimsy as gauze.

Fin forced herself to breathe slowly. It was all her imagination, she told herself. She didn't know that there were shadow monsters nearby; she was winding herself up.

She closed her eyes. She needed to sleep. If she could get to sleep, soon it would be morning and all would be well. If she could—

Something *scraped* against the ceiling of the tent.

Fin sat bolt upright, her eyes flashing wide. Her fingers sank into her sleeping bag, ready to tear herself free. Cedar remained asleep, and there was no sound from Eddie's tent besides Brie's squeaking snores.

Fin waited, her breaths sawing in and out. The air was too dry against the back of her throat. She yearned for the bottle of water next to her, but she didn't dare move. Stillness was her only refuge. Stillness and silence.

Maybe it had just been a branch in the wind. But there were no branches near enough to touch the tent.

Fin swallowed. Should she pretend to be asleep? That was her first instinct: to bury herself in her sleeping bag and pretend nothing was wrong. That was what the old Fin would have done.

But Eddie was out there. And so was Brie. And Cedar was beside her. If they were in danger, Fin had to say something.

But she couldn't quite get her voice to work. She waited another few seconds, biding her time. If she didn't hear anything, she'd go back to sleep. But if she did hear—

Something scraped slowly against the tent's frame.

Fin's stomach froze over.

Something was out there. And it wasn't human. A human would have woken Brie.

Maybe the creature was sharpening its claws. Waiting for prey to emerge.

Fin took a breath. She grabbed the flashlight; it was

heavy and made of metal, and she appreciated the heft.

Slowly, as quietly as she could, she took hold of the tent's zippered door and tugged. Inch by inch, centimeter by centimeter, she opened the tent wide enough to look out.

If it was the shadow monster, hopefully the light would drive it away. If it was something else—she'd probably start screaming. But at least that would wake the others.

Taking one last deep breath, Fin shoved her head through the gap, flicked on the flashlight, and aimed it upward.

For one brief second, the light hurt her eyes. Then she saw what sat atop her tent.

It was a raven. A small raven with a fuzzy neck and intelligent eyes.

"Morri," Fin whispered. "Were you sharpening your beak on the tentpoles?"

Morri tilted her head as if to say, *"What else would I be doing?"*

Fin glared at her. All that fear and panic because a raven liked to follow her. At least Morri hadn't woken the others.

Morri held Fin's gaze and scraped her beak against the pole a third time.

"Stop that," Fin hissed quietly.

Morri ruffled her feathers, unbothered by Fin's displeasure.

Fin scrambled out of the tent. "What are you doing here? Don't ravens sleep at night?"

Even as she said the words, Fin remembered the last time Morri had visited a human at night. The small raven had once tried to warn Mr. Madeira when there was an intruder in his home. Perhaps this wasn't a raven's idea of a prank.

Fin gazed at Morri, her anger draining away. "Is something wrong?" she whispered. "At the cottage?"

Morri fluttered her wings and looked away. Not toward the cottage, but northwest. Then she flapped into the air and alighted on a nearby branch. She looked back at Fin as if to say, *"What are you waiting for?"*

Fin grimaced. If her life were normal, she could have ignored the bird and gone back into the tent. Instead, she snatched up Cedar's flip-flops from beside the tent door, slid them on her feet, and followed a raven into the night.

She stepped carefully, so as not to snag one of the flip-flops on a fallen branch. The night was dark, quiet, and close; her every breath and movement seemed too loud. Morri flapped from branch to branch, waiting for Fin to follow. The flashlight wobbled as Fin walked. They were following a deer path. It was too faint for one of the hiking trails, but she could see the indents of cloven hooves.

Something darted across the path, and Fin jumped. The flashlight's beam fell across an opossum. Creature and girl regarded each other for a heartbeat, then the opossum scurried away.

Fin remembered her mom's warning not to go into the woods alone. She wouldn't go much farther, she promised herself. She knew all too well the fairy tales of children lost in the woods, of witches and gingerbread houses. And then there were modern stories of lost hikers, of those who thought they could navigate the wilderness and found themselves walking in circles.

She reached out and broke one of the passing fern fronds. It would mark her way back far better than a trail of breadcrumbs.

Redwood forests were old, watchful, and quiet. Alone in the woods with only a raven and a flashlight, unease prickled up the back of her neck. She did not belong here. Not at night, when the trappings of civilization receded, when the only ones who could find their way were animals.

Morri alighted on a huckleberry bush. She opened her wings, spreading them wide. Fin wasn't sure what that meant, but she froze in place. And that was when she heard the voices.

Fin hesitated, then flicked off the flashlight. She was

plunged into darkness so thick she felt as though she could reach out and touch it. Moving by memory, she inched closer to the huckleberry bushes. Morri rustled a little, and Fin followed the sound. She crouched and then gently parted the tiny huckleberry leaves, peering through them. Morri hopped onto her shoulder, talons gently pressing into the cotton of Fin's shirt.

They were looking at the old logging road. Without the trees to block out moonlight, Fin saw three figures standing on the gravel.

" . . . fix it in the post."

"There's nothing to fix. All I'm getting is a blur. I need more light."

"Why aren't we using the flashlights?"

"Because," said a woman with a pleasantly deep voice, "then I look like a star in a nineties horror flick." It was Ana Bell, Fin realized. And the rest of the SNACC Pack. They must have come out to film in the dark.

A laugh. "Only if I shoot you from the nose up."

There was a snort. "Here, use the ring light."

"Then I get the weird pupil thing."

"It's better than flashlights."

A sigh, then a man said, "I love that I went to film school so I could hold someone's phone."

"I can hold it if you don't want to." A light clicked on, illuminating the SNACC Pack. Fin blinked several times, her eyes struggling to adjust to the change.

"Oh no, I'm not letting you make me obsolete that easily." It was Michael holding the cell phone. Ana Bell wore a T-shirt with the SNACC logo; she was running her hands through her hair, as if trying to smooth it. Ryan stood off to the side, staring in the direction of the toll bridge.

Michael held the phone in one hand, while his other hand was gesturing with three fingers extended in a silent countdown. *Three, two, one—*

"Hello," said Ana Bell, and her voice was subtly different. Smoother, more enunciated. "This is the Society of North American Cryptid Chasers. As always, I am your host, Ana Bell. I'm joined by my ever-loyal brother, Ryan Bell, and the genius behind the camera, Michael Lawson. Give us a wave."

Michael gently bobbed the phone up and down.

"We're coming to you from the heart of Bigfoot country," Ana continued, and Fin could hear the capitalized B. They were here for the legend. "Northern California has long been home to tales of Sasquatch. To the north, Bluff Creek was the site of supposed film evidence and mysterious humanlike— but not human—footprints. And now we can exclusively tell you that such footprints have also appeared in Aldermere,

California." She gestured at the forest. "This small, isolated town is nearly hidden beside the redwood highway. It's known for being a hotspot of cryptid sightings. And I must confess, it's not our first time here. My brother and I first encountered Aldermere when we were teenagers, camping with our parents. Ryan even thought he saw Bigfoot . . . and after a night of terror, sure that we were about to be eaten at any moment, we emerged from our tent in the morning to find a pine tree with a few crooked branches." She paused, presumably so the viewer would have time to laugh. "When we were planning our second season, we knew we had to return to investigate the big man himself.

"But are Bigfoot sightings hoaxes? Are these tracks from a wholly different animal? Or have we found the creature that so many people claim to have glimpsed?" She lowered her voice to a soft, intimate tone, leaning toward the camera. "We're going to find out." She straightened, and her voice became more normal. "But first, a list of our most generous patrons!" She held still, her smile fixed in place for another few seconds. Then Michael lowered the phone.

"Good take," he said. "You want to pick this up in the morning?"

Ana nodded. "The tracks led northwest, so we'll go there tomorrow. It's not scheduled to rain until Tuesday night."

"I still don't know why we had to do this at night," said Michael.

"Because I look like a tourist ad in daylight," replied Ana smoothly. "And it's more authentic if we're following the tracks at all hours of the day. We'll cut the footage so it looks like we found them at night. You did get some shots of the footprints, right?"

Michael handed the phone to Ana. "I got some great footage of the ones behind the hotel. This will be even better than the Bluff Creek pictures back in the fifties."

"You do know they eventually found out the tracks in Bluff Creek were a prank?" said Ana. "Some old guy did it. After he died, it came out that he had these big carved feet in his possession. He left the tracks to scare his coworkers."

"Maybe," said Michael. "But logging equipment that weighed seven hundred pounds was moved in the night, and no one has an explanation for that. No single guy could have done it, even if he was the world's most dedicated prankster."

"Then he had friends," said Ana dismissively. "You aren't seriously telling me you believe in Bigfoot."

Michael shrugged; he wore his shoulder holster with those twin cameras clipped beneath each arm, and they swung gently as he moved. "Most of the stuff we've looked into was complete garbage. The squirroose was some taxidermy gone horribly wrong. And that chupacabra was definitely a mangy dog. But Bigfoot? There are enough eyewitness stories to make it credible."

"People don't make things credible," said Ana. "Facts make things credible." She reached down and picked up a small athletic backpack. "Come on, let's go back to the hotel. Maybe they fixed the Wi-Fi."

Michael snorted, and the two of them began gathering up their things. Fin began to rise from her own crouch, sure that there was nothing left to see, when a rustle to her right made her freeze.

Something was moving in the undergrowth. Maybe only ten or fifteen feet away. For a moment, she thought it must have been an animal, but then she realized that while she could see Ana and Michael—there was a person missing.

Ryan Bell.

He had wandered off while the others were shooting and Fin hadn't given him another thought. Had he gone into the woods to investigate things for himself?

Fin's heart slammed against her rib cage. She froze in place, too scared to move. She held her breath, pulse pounding in her ears, and waited. The rustling got louder, as if someone was approaching. Morri made a soft clicking sound with her beak. Fin was glad for the raven's presence; she wasn't alone.

But she also couldn't risk them being found. "Quiet," Fin breathed, barely moving her lips. The last thing she needed was to be discovered because her raven made a noise.

Footsteps neared Fin's hiding place. One, and then two, and Fin could hear someone breathing. She pressed a hand to her mouth and nose and thought, *Don't come closer, don't come closer, just keep going—*

Fin chanced a look up and saw Ryan Bell perhaps five feet away, his cell phone in hand, light falling across the row of huckleberry bushes. Fin held her breath as the flashlight's beam drifted through the undergrowth. Fin glanced over her shoulder and saw what Ryan was staring at.

There was a broken fern frond about ten feet behind Fin. One of the ferns *she* had broken, because she had no other way to mark her path. It hung there, fresh and green. And a few feet behind that was another broken frond. Fin's trail of broken ferns led all the way back to her small campsite—and the bigfoot sleeping there.

Fin's fear churned in her stomach. Perhaps Ryan would realize that an animal couldn't have been so deliberate about trampled greenery. A deer would have slipped through without disturbing a leaf, while a bear would have trampled all in its path. Only a human would have broken a single frond and walked away.

Humans could choose what they broke.

She should have found a different way to mark her path.

Fin's lungs were burning as Ryan looked at the damaged undergrowth. He was going to find her. He would trace the small trail to where she crouched with her raven, and demand to know why she'd followed them. They might even insist on taking her home, and then Mom would find out, and—

Ryan turned back toward the logging road. He pushed through the huckleberries, stepping out onto the gravel.

"Call of nature?" asked Michael.

Ryan shook his head. "Thought I saw something. There are more tracks out here, you know. We should come back tomorrow."

"Really?" Michael took a step toward the huckleberry bushes.

Fin swallowed hard. She willed them to stay away, to *leave*. Her legs were starting to burn from holding a crouch for so long.

"Come on," said Ana. Her voice held an easy authority. "The last thing we need is to go blundering into the woods to be attacked by a cougar or something. The nearest hospital is like three hours away."

"An hour and a half," said Michael. "But I do see your point."

"I love that you memorized where the nearest ER is, but you forgot a toothbrush," said Ana.

"Priorities," said Michael.

The three of them fell into an easy and familiar banter as they gathered up their things. Fin watched, her heartbeat slowing, as the SNACC Pack walked in the direction of town. Still, she didn't move. Only once they turned a corner did Fin allow herself to rise. Her knees ached.

It was one thing to know that there was a film crew poking around Aldermere, but it was another to see them in action. Fin wanted to put her arms around the town, to shield it from view so long as SNACC was trying to uncover its secrets.

Morri made a soft clicking sound, and Fin reached up to stroke the feathers beneath her beak. "Thanks for the heads-up," she whispered. Without the raven, Fin would never have known the film crew was so near the campsite.

Morri croaked, pleased with herself.

"You think they're trouble too?" asked Fin. She wasn't sure if the raven understood her. But Morri spread her wings and flew into the air, vanishing into the night.

Fin returned to the campsite on her own, flicking on the flashlight once she was sure no one was near enough to see it. She picked her way back using the trail of broken ferns, all the while wishing she'd worn different shoes than borrowed flip-flops; they weren't built for espionage. Finally she emerged from the woods into the small clearing. Two blue tents sat squat and silent. Fin slipped out of the shoes and unzipped the tent as quietly as she could.

Cedar hadn't roused. Her face was relaxed in sleep, dark hair spilling across her pillow. Fin hastily flicked off the flashlight and made her way to her own sleeping bag. As she crawled inside, her fingers touched something hard and cold on her pillow. Fin flinched in surprise. Had a rock gotten into the tent?

Fin picked up the strange object, chancing one more use of the flashlight to see it.

Silver gleaned between her fingers. A slender threaded chain—and a locket.

It was the locket she had admired so much at the Foragers' Market, still complete with its hand-labeled forty-five-dollar price tag.

Fin's mouth went dry. For one dizzying moment, she wondered if she'd accidentally taken it and it had fallen out of her pocket. But she had never stolen anything in her life—well, except for a single packet of matches from Mrs. Brackenbury. And, technically, some magical tea. But beyond that, Fin had always lived in fear of what might happen if she broke the rules.

The locket swung from her fingers, pretty and so very not hers.

She hadn't taken it. She *knew* she hadn't taken it.

So how had it ended up on her pillow? It couldn't have been Morri; she couldn't get inside the tent. And Fin would have seen her carrying a locket.

Fin turned off the flashlight, the locket squeezed in her hand.

TEN
Things Found in the Woods

Morning smelled of damp earth and hot cinnamon buns.

Fin cupped her breakfast with both hands, letting the warmth sink into her cold fingers. Steam rose from the buttery swirls of pastry and sugar. Cedar had retrieved them from Brewed Awakening; she'd also taken the time to check in with her parents and cheerfully inform them she was spending another day at Fin's cottage.

In reality, she would be babysitting Brie with a bag of bread and apples and a deck of cards to keep herself occupied.

Fin and Eddie told Mom they'd be spending the day at the cottage too. But that was slightly untrue. They did spend an hour at the cottage—and then once Mom left for work, Fin and Eddie set off down Redwood Street toward the eastern hiking trails.

"You think Cedar will be okay with Brie?" asked Eddie.

Fin tore off a small bit of bun and popped it into her mouth. It melted on her tongue. "Yeah, I think so. She didn't seem worried. And Cedar likes animals."

Brie had woken with the dawn, making soft meeping sounds until Fin and Cedar stumbled blearily out of their tent and retrieved a granola bar for her. Eddie, who had never been a morning person, had stayed in his sleeping bag and looked vaguely offended at the sun for daring to rise so early.

Fin had told them about the SNACC Pack. Cedar had been more troubled than Eddie, a frown creasing her mouth. "You think they'll follow the tracks here?" she had asked anxiously. "Since they already investigated the ones near the inn?"

"If you hear anyone approach, move Brie to the cottage," Fin answered. "Mom's at work until four."

Brie had been content to eat the granola bar while leaning against Fin, gazing up at her with puppy-eyed adoration. Fin chanced a scratch behind the bigfoot's ears, and Brie closed her eyes in pleasure.

Fin knew she should not get attached to the baby

bigfoot. Brie wasn't a pet. She wasn't going to stay. She was a problem that needed to be solved.

But she was a very cute problem.

Fin hadn't told the others about the locket she'd found on her pillow. It felt like something secretive and shameful. She didn't know how to explain how she had it. For all of Aldermere's weirdness, objects hadn't ever followed people around. She'd crammed the locket into one of the zipped pockets inside her coat. She should return it to the woman at the Foragers' Market next weekend. But how to do so without anyone noticing?

"So where are we going?" asked Fin, trying to distract herself.

Eddie pulled a crumpled sheet of paper from his pocket. "Well, Nick gave us three places to check. The closest one is a grove of trees near where Bower's Creek touches the river."

"Do we have to get across the river?" asked Fin. "I don't think there's a way except the old toll bridge. And we're not supposed to use it."

"No," said Eddie. "The bigfoot spot is on the south side of the river."

"Is the plural of bigfoot 'bigfoots' or 'bigfeet'?" she asked.

Eddie shrugged. "Dunno. Maybe it's like 'moose' and

the plural's the same as the singular. Or you could ask the English teacher at school."

They picked up a hiking trail behind the inn. Fin glanced at the dumpsters; Brie's tracks would probably have been trampled by those carrying out garbage, and Eddie seemed confident with Nick's notes, so they walked by without investigating. There was a brown metal sign, with the trail's length and a small map. An older couple was nearby, checking the contents of a backpack. Fin and Eddie nodded politely.

Fin had never been much of a hiker; she liked the trails and seeing the forest, but the idea of spending all day climbing up a hill was more daunting than enjoyable. The sunshine was bright today, and Fin had a feeling the afternoon would be a warm one. The shift from misty spring mornings to hot and dry summers was coming a little earlier every year.

Eddie took the lead, and Fin was content to follow. He set a brisk pace, but since Fin's legs were a few inches longer than his, she kept up easily. "Do the bigfoots prefer our forest?" asked Fin. This was a question that had been nagging at her since last night, when she'd overheard SNACC. "Because I heard Ana Bell talking about tracks being seen near Bluff Creek in the fifties."

The trail wound up a hill, twisting back and forth so that the incline wasn't too steep. Five-fingered ferns protruded from the hillside and a fat squirrel watched them, tail whipping back and forth.

"That is the question, isn't it?" Eddie said thoughtfully. "I'm not exactly sure. I think—and this is a theory, remember—that bigfoots like old forests. There used to be a lot more before logging went big. That is why there've been some sightings all over the Pacific Northwest: people would cut into the bigfoots' territory and see tracks. Or maybe the bigfoots were investigating what happened to their homes."

"Nick said they can smell people like wolves do," said Fin. "That's how they manage to stay unseen. But they don't mind kids. So most of the real bigfoot sightings are kids catching a glimpse."

"Well," said Eddie, "that explains why everyone still thinks they're a myth. Who's going to believe a kid?"

They came to the top of the hill and paused for a moment, looking back at Aldermere. The town was tiny from this angle, hidden by branches. Eddie turned to continue along the trail. Fin gave the familiar buildings one last glance before following.

The hiking trail was well marked, with plenty of signs reminding tourists not to leave it. Some of the warnings were about bears and cougars, while others stated that endangered wildlife could be disturbed by intruders. Fin and Eddie followed the trail for a good half hour, winding through old-growth forest. The thick trees blotted out the sunshine, casting the world into a morning twilight. Fin was glad she'd brought her army surplus coat. The coat was old and heavy, like armor. She was a little braver while wearing it. Not that they were in a dangerous wilderness; they passed a family having a breakfast picnic with two young children, a woman with a brochure on bird identification and a pair of binoculars hanging from around her neck, and a man huffing as he pushed a pug up the hill in a stroller. "Doesn't that defeat the purpose of taking a dog for a walk?" asked Eddie, once the man was out of earshot.

Fin shrugged. "I think Mr. Bull likes his stroller walks, but I don't know. The closest thing I have to a pet is a raven who likes to wake me up in the middle of the night."

The trail turned, but Eddie didn't follow it. Here, the undergrowth thinned out. He glanced from side to side to make sure no one was nearby to see them; then he slipped off the trail and into the woods. Fin swallowed, feeling that old twinge of anxiety at the thought of rule breaking. They were supposed to keep to the trails. But finding Brie's family mattered more. She straightened her shoulders and followed Eddie.

In a few steps, Fin found herself in a world of redwood

sorrel and sword ferns. The shade from the canopy of the old-growth redwoods prevented much of the undergrowth from flourishing, which made it easier to traverse the forest. There were no blackberry or huckleberry bushes to tug at her clothes, and no poison oak to shy away from—not even smaller trees. The old redwoods were thick as cars, tall and proud. The reverent silence reminded Fin a little of churches or chapels; even the animals respected the quiet.

Eddie picked his way carefully through the forest. He always knew where to set his feet so as not to disturb the plants, and Fin tried to follow in his footsteps. They walked for another twenty minutes, until Fin heard the distinct trickle of running water. Eddie stepped to one side, making room for her, and Fin found herself at the edge of Bower's Creek.

It was a beautiful creek—clear water running over mossy stones, with swirls and eddies near fallen branches. But both knew better than to reach down and trail their fingers through the water. Fin had a few crumbs left over from her cinnamon bun, and she tossed them into the water.

The crumbs bobbed cheerily in the stream. The current tugged them into the shadows and—

A gray-green hand, the fingers pricked with claws, reached up and dragged the crumbs beneath the surface.

It happened so quickly that Fin might have missed it if she had blinked. She flinched, and even Eddie retreated a step.

"Well," she said, "we're not crossing here."

They turned and followed the edge of the water. No one knew precisely what lived in Bower's Creek—theories ranged from a vengeful mermaid to a miniature kraken. Sunlight played across the rippling water, and something in the movement reminded Fin of the eerie grace of the shadow monster stealing across the lawn.

She glanced at the shadows all around: the long ones cast by redwoods, the jagged silhouettes of ferns, and even the tiny, flickering shadows cast by the small fish swimming in the creek. She thought of Nick saying that one way to avoid a shadow was to go somewhere too dark to cast one. "What if the shadow monster is nearby?" she said in a low tone. "You think it might also be looking for the bigfoot herd?"

Eddie's mouth scrunched to one side. "Not sure. I don't know anything about shadow monsters. I've never even heard of anything like that."

"We don't know everything about magic," said Fin. "I mean, neither of us knew about tea monsters before last fall."

"Very true," admitted Eddie.

Fin said, "Okay, so if shadow monsters are a thing, why is it showing up now?"

"What do you mean?"

"I mean," said Fin, "things that usually stay out of town are coming *into* town. A baby bigfoot. Shadow creatures. *Nick.*"

Eddie snorted. "Okay, you've got a point."

"Something in Aldermere has changed," said Fin. "Why else would this be happening?"

Eddie hummed quietly to himself for a few steps. Then he said, "Or something's changed outside of it."

"What do you mean?" Fin stepped around a large root protruding from the ground.

"I mean," said Eddie, "what if monsters are coming into town because there's something even scarier out there?" He gestured at the expanse of forest.

Unbidden, Fin's gaze fell to the water again. She thought of monsters both seen and unseen. And of all the things that could still lurk within the depths of the old woods.

"Well," she said, "I guess the only question is . . . what are monsters afraid of?"

Bower's Creek wound through the forest, toward a fork in the Eel River. The undergrowth was a little thicker by the creek;

there were brambles and wildflowers that had to be gently pushed aside or stepped over. Fin was glad for the thick material of her coat when a blackberry thorn snagged in her sleeve. Eddie found several snakes sunning themselves on rocks and pointed each out, naming its species and what it ate. She knew Eddie's chatter was good for warding off bears and other dangerous wildlife, but she only half listened, most of her attention on the forest. She kept looking for footprints like Brie's, for broken branches, for any indication that a bigfoot might have passed this way.

As they drew closer to the place on Nick's list, Eddie's chitchat faded away. He moved with more purpose, angling himself so that no branches would break beneath his sneakers. Fin tried to mimic him, and she winced every time a fern frond rustled against her jeans. The whisper of the creek became more raucous, water rushing over larger rocks. They rounded a bend, and Fin saw the river. It wasn't that big—a stretch of water about thirty-five feet across, the deceptively clear water making it appear shallow. But Mom had warned them never to cross without an adult; the currents could be strong, and it was deep enough to drown in if a person was caught unawares. There was an old, rusted NO FISHING sign that bore the remnants of a bird's nest.

Eddie scanned the place where the river met the creek.

There was a stretch of muddy bank and he knelt beside it, touching the dirt with his bare fingers.

"Are you trying to talk to it?" asked Fin, only sort of joking.

Eddie flicked the mud from his fingers, then wiped the remnants on his shirt. "It's damp enough that we should see tracks, if there are any."

There weren't. They spent a good twenty minutes walking alongside the river, looking for any signs that a bigfoot herd might have passed by. But if there were any clues, neither Fin nor Eddie spotted them. The sun was high, and it warmed the back of Fin's neck. She'd tied her hair back this morning, too busy to bother showering. But now she felt sweaty and dirty from the hike, and the cool, clean water of a shower sounded wonderful.

"Is anything here?" she finally said.

Eddie was frowning, lines scrunched in his forehead as he studied the river. "I don't think so," he admitted. "I . . . I don't get the sense anything's passed by here for a while."

Fin nodded. That was good enough for her. "Then let's go back. I don't want to leave Cedar and Brie alone for too long, in case something happens."

"Yeah." Eddie sounded frustrated. Finding animals was his specialty. Not finding the bigfoot herd on the first try wasn't a big deal to her, but it mattered to Eddie.

She reached out and put a hand on his arm. "We'll get Brie back to her family."

Eddie looked at her. "You sound pretty sure about that."

Fin wasn't sure of many things—her anxiety made the entire world into a "maybe" or a "what if." But Eddie was one of the few people she knew she could depend on. "If anyone can find Brie's family, you can."

They headed back toward town. Eddie led them by a different trail, picking up one of the older hiking paths. It was more overgrown, less polished, and Fin knew that Eddie hoped to see some sign of the bigfoot herd. But the only thing they found was a tourist with an unleashed dog heading toward Bower's Creek. Fin glanced pointedly at one of the PLEASE LEASH YOUR ANIMAL signs that were scattered alongside the path, but Eddie was braver.

"You'll get ticketed if a park ranger sees your dog without a leash!" he called. The tourist, a middle-aged man, looked up. Irritation flashed across his face.

Fin flushed, even though she wasn't the one who'd spoken up. Secondhand embarrassment for Eddie's boldness.

"There aren't any park rangers in town," she murmured, once they were out of earshot.

"Yeah, but he doesn't know that," said Eddie. He shook

his head, disapproving. "Five bucks says that dog gets eaten. We only gave the Bower's Creek monster a few crumbs. It's got to be hungry."

Fin's stomach rumbled. "So am I." The small cinnamon bun had taken the edge off, but she yearned for a more substantial meal.

They left the hiking trail behind, pushing through overhanging branches until they stood on Main Street. Brewed Awakening was bustling, all its outdoor tables crowded. Across the street, on Fin's right, was the small rental house where River and his family were still settling in. Broken-down cardboard boxes were lined up beside the small redwood fence, and a few full boxes were stacked up beside the front door. River himself was on the steps of the house, his face scrunched up as he looked down at a cell phone. There wouldn't be any service, but maybe he was playing a game. As Fin and Eddie passed by, River's gaze rose to meet them. Fin gave him the smallest of waves, but he didn't return it.

Mrs. Brackenbury and Talia were sitting outside. Mrs. Brackenbury had a swinging bench attached to her porch awning, and she liked to take her coffee there so she could talk to the passersby. Mr. Bull was asleep on one of the porch steps. "Eddie, Finley," Mrs. Brackenbury called. "How are you?"

Fin felt the familiar squirm of guilt when her eyes landed on Talia. But she knew they couldn't walk away without answering. Reluctantly, she walked up the stone path to the porch. "Good," said Eddie. "How're you?"

Sitting between the two women was a small tray of tea and scones smeared with olallieberry jam.

"We've been watching the internet show people wander through town," said Talia. "They have to pass by here to get back to the inn."

"I overheard them talking about needing the internet," said Mrs. Brackenbury. "The blond boy was complaining about that at Brewed Awakening."

"I bet they didn't give them the password, right?" said Eddie, grinning.

"Nope," said Fin.

"I feel a bit sorry for them," said Mrs. Brackenbury. "I saw the girl with the green hair wandering through town with her phone like she was hoping for a signal."

"She'd need to walk twenty miles south for that," said Talia. She cut a sharp look at Fin. "And where have you two been?"

Fin realized her boots were muddy. "We—uh. We went for a hike in the woods."

Talia's mouth curled up at one corner. Her lipstick was

a bright reddish orange, and it was always impeccable. "I thought the two of you might be following that film crew around," she said. "You are rather good at guarding Aldermere from those who want to exploit it." She brought a cup of tea to her lips, and her knowing gaze held Fin's as she took a sip. The tea would be just tea. The magic mortar that Talia needed to enchant tea had been lost with the tea shop.

Talia was the only adult who knew the truth about what had happened last fall. Fin had thought she deserved the whole story behind why her home had vanished—after all, Talia had paid the steepest price to keep Aldermere safe.

"Pretty sure they're not going to be impressed by a couple of kids," said Eddie.

Mrs. Brackenbury laughed. "If they'd visited Redfern back in the day, they'd have ended up with flat tires or their film mysteriously missing."

Fin gaped at Mrs. Brackenbury. "I—I'm pretty sure most of their cameras don't use film anymore," was all she could think to say.

Eddie didn't hold back. "You slashed visitors' tires?" he said, impressed.

"I never said *I* did," replied Mrs. Brackenbury. "But intrusive visitors always found themselves . . . well. They didn't stay for long. Too many little annoyances would crop up."

It wasn't the first time Fin had heard Mrs. Brackenbury talk about Redfern. Supposedly the town that predated Aldermere had been wilder, more dangerous.

"Perhaps if this were Redfern, things would be better protected," Talia murmured, almost to herself. "We certainly wouldn't be having all these outsiders move into town."

"How are the new neighbors?" asked Fin quietly, with a glance toward River's front yard.

"We haven't seen them much," said Talia. "The parents have been driving back and forth a few times a day, moving stuff in. I think the boy has been wandering around a little. I saw him skulking around Brewed Awakening this morning."

"Well," said Eddie darkly, "hopefully no one gives him the Wi-Fi password either."

Fin nudged him. "Mean."

"I'm not mean, he's mean," protested Eddie.

"He's mad River kept winning the science fair until last year," Fin said to Mrs. Brackenbury and Talia.

"Well, everyone needs competition," said Mrs. Brackenbury. "So long as you don't end up feeding him to Bower's Creek, rivalry can be healthy."

Eddie scowled.

Mrs. Brackenbury sent them off with a scone apiece, and Fin gave Mr. Bull a scratch behind his ears. She glanced over her shoulder and saw River all alone on the steps of his house, his eyes following them. She looked away quickly.

They made their way back to the big house, through the backyard, past the cottage, and toward their small campsite. Fin ate half her scone and kept the rest for Brie.

Together they rounded the fallen log and stepped into the clearing. To Fin's relief, all seemed well. The tents were intact and untouched. Cedar was sitting on the ground, talking quietly to Brie. Cedar reached down to ruffle her ears, and Brie made a soft meeping sound, leaning against Cedar's knee.

"Did you find anything?" Cedar asked eagerly.

Fin plopped herself down on the fallen log. "A lot of muddy trails. Ferns. The Bower's Creek monster."

Cedar nodded sympathetically. "Well, there are more places on that list Nick gave you, right? We'll keep looking."

Brie walked toward Eddie, sniffing around his fingers. He absentmindedly patted her on the head. Brie looked vaguely annoyed, as if she'd been expecting a treat instead of petting.

"There's one east of town," said Eddie. "We can try

that this afternoon, after I get some lunch." As if on cue, his stomach grumbled loudly. "I think I'm gonna go to the cottage and make a sandwich."

"Make two," replied Fin. "Or maybe three." She turned to Cedar. "You hungry?"

The question seemed to stump Cedar. She didn't answer for a few moments, her fingers twisting around each other. She opened her mouth, then nothing emerged. Her eyes widened with fear, and Fin suddenly went cold. Cedar never looked panicked.

A twig snapped behind Fin. She twisted around, swinging one leg over the log.

It took her eyes a moment to see the figure in the shadow of a redwood tree.

It was River.

River stood only twenty feet away, looking as shocked as though someone had hit him with cold water. One foot was lifted and held in midair, waiting to be set down. But he didn't move. He was staring into the campsite, his gaze fixed on Brie.

Fin couldn't move either. The breath was caught in her lungs; anything she might have wanted to say crumbled on her tongue.

Finally River put his foot down. It slipped on one of the

roots and he barely caught himself. But he didn't notice. He kept staring at Brie.

"What *is* that thing?" he said, mouth agape.

"River?" said Fin. Her voice quavered on his name. "What—what are you doing here?"

"I—I wanted to use your phone," said River numbly. He swallowed several times. "You said I could . . ." He took a step back.

"The phone?" asked Eddie, confused. "You think we have one out *here*?"

River retreated another step.

"Scott," said Cedar, holding out a beseeching hand. "Wait."

But River didn't wait. He turned, stumbled over the root a second time, and then tore off toward the cottage.

"No!" Cedar rushed after him.

Fin barely had time to think. She threw herself after them. It wasn't easy to run in a forest—there were too many things to trip over—but that didn't stop her. Ferns whipped at her legs, and she had to leap over the fallen log. She could hear Cedar ahead, calling out to River. Eddie was somewhere behind her.

"Stop! Scott, please!"

Fear flooded Fin's body as she ran. River had seen Brie.

He'd seen the bigfoot. He wouldn't keep her a secret—he'd probably go right to his parents and tell them about the monster in the woods.

Fin forced her legs to pump even faster. She couldn't let this happen. She wouldn't.

She raced around a tree and nearly slammed into Cedar. The other girl had come to a halt, and River stood only a few feet away. For a moment, Fin thought that Cedar must have gotten through to him. Made him understand that he couldn't keep running, that he had to listen.

Then she saw the shifting darkness.

The shadow coalesced into the vague shape of a horse. It rose up, looking like something made of magic and spilled ink, its edges wavering and unsure. It stood over River, head lowered like it might charge.

The shadow monster. It wasn't lurking in the woods or hunting bigfoots—it was here.

A fresh burn of panic swept through Fin. She scrambled for the flashlight. She'd shoved it into her heavy coat pocket, and her fingers curled around the cold metal. She drew it out, fumbling to twist the light to life. But her sweaty fingers slipped, and the flashlight fell to the ground.

"Wait," said Cedar. She stepped forward, toward River

and the shadow. Fin uttered a wordless cry of warning, wanting to reach for her, to pull her back to safety.

But before Fin could touch her, Cedar laid her hand across the shadow's nose. "It's okay," she whispered. "It's okay, it's okay." For a moment Fin thought Cedar was trying to reassure River—but she realized the other girl was speaking to the monster.

And then Fin saw that Cedar cast no shadow.

None at all.

ELEVEN
Forgotten and Unforgotten

For a long moment, no one moved. To Fin, it seemed as though the very forest was holding its breath.

Then River made a noise.

It wasn't a very dignified noise—it was a strangled whimper that belonged to a creature far smaller than Scott River. He scuttled backward on all fours until he hit a tree. His fingers scrabbled at the rough bark, as if he needed its solidity. His gaze never left the monstrous, shadowy creature standing by Cedar.

Eddie skidded to a halt beside Fin, his breathing hard and gaze wide with alarm. He seized Fin's sleeve, as if he was prepared to run and take her with him. "What is that thing?"

"It's okay," said Cedar. Her voice came out frantic, words tripping over each other.

Fin gaped at Cedar. She tried to cobble a sentence together, but all she could manage was "What?"

"It's mine," said Cedar. "I'm sorry, I wanted to tell you."

The shadow monster was cast by *Cedar*. But that couldn't be true. Cedar was normal—well, normal for Aldermere. She helped her parents with the coffee shop; she was quiet in school; she liked animals and was polite to everyone she met. This monstrous creature was nothing like Cedar.

"It isn't real," said River, his words jamming together. "That—that big-footed thing isn't real. That shadow isn't real. You're doing it, somehow. It's special effects, holograms—"

The shadow took a step closer, eyed him with a distinctly horselike tilt of its head, and then reached down to tug at his shoelaces with its teeth.

River made a sound like a dog whose tail had been stepped on.

"It's all real," said Cedar. She patted the horse's neck, and it took a step back from River. Cedar's gaze met Fin's. "The other night, she must have been following Brie, investigating the herd of bigfoots. She likes to keep track of the other magical creatures. It's how I knew about the tracks in town."

Fin's memories were a tangle of yarn, and pulling on

this one thread could unravel everything. She thought of how Cedar knew things about people, and how she'd once explained that she was observant. She thought of Cedar's silence when Fin had told her and Eddie about the shadow monster she'd glimpsed. And then she thought of another night, nearly six months before.

"In the fall, before the science fair," she said faintly. "Teafin warned me to stay indoors because something scary was outside the house. Was that . . . was that your shadow? Was it watching me, even back then?"

Cedar's gaze fell to the ground between them. Shame crossed her face. "I mean, I didn't tell her to. But yeah, that was probably my shadow."

For a heartbeat, anger swelled within Fin. It was like a match being struck—a brief moment of heat. Cedar had lied to her. All this time, Cedar had lied—if not through her words, then through her lack of them. She could have told Fin and Eddie about her shadow monster at any time in the last six months, and she'd never said. Not a thing.

And then, as abruptly as it had flared, Fin's anger was doused. Because Cedar looked *terrified*. Her shoulders were pulled tight, her mouth drawn and her fingers shaking. She looked as though she was bracing herself for Fin to call her a monster too.

And Fin remembered her conversation with Nick. *"I don't think I want to meet whatever could cast a shadow like that."*

Nick had said, *"Maybe, maybe not."*

Had he known? Guessed? Fin didn't know.

One last thing Fin knew: Cedar was her friend. She'd always stood by Fin, even when things were dangerous. She could have walked away, but she hadn't. Cedar was kind and good, and Fin refused to believe otherwise until she had absolute proof.

"How did this happen?" asked Fin.

Cedar's voice wobbled. "The old toll bridge."

Eddie blinked. "But we're not supposed to use it."

"Well, I know that *now*," said Cedar. "But when my family first moved here, no one trusted us. So they kept all the rules secret."

Fin drew in a sharp breath. She could see where this was going. "You crossed."

"Yes," said Cedar. "I was seven and I didn't understand. No one does, until they pay the price."

"What *is* the price?" asked Eddie. He took a step closer to the shadow, his curiosity overriding common sense.

Cedar lifted her chin. "The thing you most desperately want. It'll give it to you, if you cross. You don't even have to utter the words—it'll know." She glanced at the shadow. "I was lonely. So lonely. I wanted friends in Aldermere, people I could talk to and hang out with. When I was walking home, I was entertaining myself by making shadow puppets on the gravel road." She held up one hand, cupped like a bird's head. "You've made shadows like this, right?"

"Doesn't everyone?" Fin could recall a few times she and Eddie had tried to make increasingly weird shadow shapes with a flashlight when they were bored.

Cedar smiled briefly, but it fell away. "Yeah. It was a sunny day and I was walking back toward town, the sun at my shoulder, and I used both hands to make a horse shadow puppet. Just for fun, you know? But the second I cast it, the shadow rose up and came alive. And she looks like . . . well, a monster, because I'm really, really bad at shadow puppets."

The shadow dipped its head, as if in agreement.

"But she's not bad," said Cedar. Her voice faltered, as if her own convictions weren't as strong as she wished. "I mean, I don't think she's bad. I hope she isn't."

"So you wished for friends," said Fin, "and the toll bridge gave you a shadow monster?"

"I'm not getting why that's a bad thing," said Eddie, forehead scrunching. "If the bridge grants wishes, then why's everyone warned away from it?"

Cedar met Fin's gaze. Her face had gone a little sad. "You haven't figured it out by now?"

Fin shook her head.

Cedar said, "I was lonely. I wanted a friend. And I got one. But now, unless someone believes in magic, they won't notice me. They won't even see me."

Fin scrunched up her forehead in confusion. "What? No, you aren't invisible."

"They see me," said Cedar. "For a moment. They'll talk to me. But when they look away, I'm an afterthought. The first time we met, you asked for my name. Did you remember it afterward?"

Fin flushed. "I'm bad with names," she said. "And directions. It had nothing to do with you."

"It had everything to do with me," said Cedar. "Anyone who doesn't believe in magic won't think about me. They won't know me. I'm the girl at the coffee shop, or that girl who sits behind Evan in geography, or that one girl who eats alone. I'm a placeholder, defined by the things around me. You didn't remember my name until you believed in Aldermere, in magic." She swallowed. "The locals know me, but there aren't that many kids here in Aldermere. Eddie was nice, but he's always busy helping some animal. The Reyes twins have each other. Everyone else already had friends. So I was alone, except for my shadow."

Old mysteries were suddenly making sense—why Cedar, who was pretty and friendly and polite, never had any friends at school, or how she'd guessed about Teafin faster than anyone else. This even explained why River could never remember Cedar's name. It wasn't rudeness; it was magic.

"But then you helped me last fall," said Fin. "And we became friends."

Cedar nodded. "I should have told you then, but I didn't. Because I was scared that you would think I was weird."

Fin snorted. "I had a doppelgänger made of tea running around. I'm not exactly normal either."

"That's the first thing that made me think we could be friends, honestly," said Cedar, with a weary little smile. "You were always so . . . reserved. I thought maybe you weren't looking for any friends besides Eddie."

Fin thought about Cedar—or rather, all the times she hadn't thought about Cedar: how she'd been Coffee Shop Girl for several months in Fin's head, and then Fin had only ever thought about her when she'd visited Brewed Awakening or passed her in the hallways at school. It made Fin squirm with shame; she should've noticed Cedar.

"How many people have crossed?" asked Eddie, his mind clearly still on the toll bridge.

Cedar shrugged one shoulder. "No idea. The old logging road's a dead end, so it's not like a lot of people walk up that way. But it's probably quite a few tourists who never realize, and then they leave Aldermere and the magic fades, after a while."

A wave of cold swept through Fin. She thought of that chain with the NO TRESPASSING sign strung across the bridge. Of how easy it would be to step over that chain, to set foot on the old redwood bridge. Nick had been right at the town meeting—ignorance wasn't protection. It hadn't protected Cedar.

"You're lying."

The words jerked Fin from her thoughts with a dizzying abruptness. She turned toward River. He had stepped away from the tree, one shoelace still undone. His face was blanched of all color, but his eyes were flinty. His glasses had slipped down his nose and he didn't seem to notice.

"This is all some trick," he said hotly. "This place, this town—you're all doing it on purpose to make tourists think it's real. But magic . . ." He stumbled over the word. "Isn't real. I don't know what you're doing or how you're doing it, but I'm going to find out." He took a step closer to Cedar, his finger pointed at her. "You're a freak, like the rest of them—"

It happened so fast, Fin's eyes almost couldn't follow the

motion. The shadow horse whipped its head, its mane flying out like tendrils of dark cobwebs.

River's hand jerked back and he stumbled, a cry wrenching from his lips. He pressed his hand to his chest and Fin saw the thin cut across his knuckles. Blood welled up, and he gazed down at the small wound as if he couldn't believe it.

"Penny, no!" Cedar took hold of the shadow horse's nose, stroking back and forth. "Calm down. You're okay, we're okay—"

The horse was scared, Fin realized. It had lashed out in fear when River threatened it.

And Fin remembered something Cedar had said a long time ago.

"Monsters are only monstrous until you befriend them."

"Hey," said Fin, stepping forward. She extended her hand, palm out. She tried to keep her voice low and calm, the way Nick spoke to the ravens. "Shh, we're all friends here."

The horse went still. It did not have eyes—but Fin had the impression its attention was on her. She tentatively walked closer and laid her hand on the horse's cheek. To her surprise, the creature was warm and soft as suede beneath her fingertips. "See, nothing to be scared of," said Fin.

"Can I touch her?" asked Eddie, as if he couldn't bear to be the only person not petting the shadow horse.

Cedar sucked in a breath, startled by the question. "I—yes. It's fine."

Eddie walked forward and patted the horse's shoulder. "Hey there. You're not scary at all, are you?"

The horse lowered its head, as if relaxed. And then it suddenly melted away beneath Fin's hand. It floated through her fingers like smoke, formless and insubstantial, draining downward. Before Fin could speak a word, the shadow horse pooled onto the ground—into the form of Cedar's shadow. They all looked at it for a few heartbeats. Eddie squatted down and poked the shadow. It didn't move.

It was just a shadow again.

Fin looked over her shoulder. "River, you okay?"

But when Fin's gaze fell on the place where River had crouched, she froze in surprise.

The spot was empty.

"Where'd . . ." Fin began to say, unable to finish.

There was no sign of him, except for the places in the needles where his shoes had scuffed into the dirt. Fin turned in a full circle.

River was gone.

TWELVE
Unvarnished Truths and Floors

"Why was he even here?" asked Eddie.

They had returned to the campsite. Brie had been waiting for them, her whiskers pointed forward and quivering nervously. Fin gave her the last half of the scone to reassure her. Brie carried the pastry a few feet away, as if worried someone might try to take it from her, then began nibbling at it.

Fin sat on the rotted log with Cedar beside her, and Eddie was cross-legged on the ground. Fin said, "It was my fault. I told him that if he wanted to call his friends, he could use the landline at the cottage."

Eddie gaped at her. "Why?"

"Because I felt sorry for him," said Fin defensively. "I'd found out he lost his home and he couldn't even call his friends. I didn't think he would follow us to the campsite."

Eddie pinched the bridge of his nose. "You know what they say about good deeds."

"They are their own reward?"

"They never go unpunished," replied Eddie. "That's why Mom never gives out tarot freebies. She says it's bad luck."

"And what about Scott's hand?" asked Cedar. Her fingers were tightly clasped over her knees, and she hunched her shoulders. "He was bleeding."

"It looked like a paper cut," said Eddie. "Not that bad."

"But it *could* have been." Cedar clutched at her own arms. "Penny's normally not violent, but—"

"Penny?" asked Fin.

Cedar met her eyes. "Penumbra," she said. "Another word for shadow."

"Well, it's less of a mouthful than 'shadow-horse monster thing,'" said Eddie. "Penny it is."

Fin looked down at Cedar's shadow. It was human shaped and moved only when Cedar did. "Can you control it—I mean, her?"

Cedar gave a little shrug. "Not really. I can summon her. And if I try hard, I can sometimes make her go away.

But most of the time she just . . . wakes up. It took me a few months to realize that she's awake when I'm dreaming. Things would move around my bedroom when I was asleep. She might knock over a glass of water. When I have bad dreams, it's worse. Sometimes our garden would be torn up or the neighbors would complain about bears knocking over their garbage. But it was her."

"And no one's ever noticed a shadow horse running around while you sleep?" asked Eddie.

Cedar raised her brows. "Did *you* notice last night?"

"No," he said, unashamed. "But to be fair, I was sleeping while a baby bigfoot tried to snuggle up to me. She snores, by the way."

That got a smile out of Cedar.

"I didn't either," said Fin quietly. She thought of when she had left the tent last night. She hadn't noticed if Cedar's shadow had looked normal. Or if she'd had one at all.

After all, who would look for a shadow in the dark?

"No one's ever put it together," said Cedar. "And I wasn't going to tell anyone."

"Not your parents?" asked Fin. "I mean, they seem nice and—"

Cedar slid her a significant look. "Like you told your mom about Teafin?"

That stopped Fin cold.

Because it was true. She had never told Mom about her tea doppelgänger. And for a heartbeat, Fin wanted to protest that her situation had been different. Mom was frightened of magic, reluctant to come to Aldermere. She'd only returned to town because Fin's father had been stalking them and they'd needed a safe place to stay. But Cedar's parents were both nice, and they believed in magic. Surely it wouldn't be so bad to confide in them.

But then Fin remembered the fear and the shame of last fall. Fin had gone to the tea shop to fix a perceived flaw within herself, using the magical tea to make herself braver. And instead she'd accidentally created a monster.

Cedar had gone to the bridge yearning for friends.

Maybe loneliness was a little like fear. It crept into a person's life and filled up all the empty spaces until it was difficult to breathe.

Fin didn't like talking about her anxiety with anyone she didn't know; perhaps Cedar hadn't wanted to admit that she'd had a hard time making friends, that she'd craved something no one offered freely. Better to smile and remain at the coffee shop, working alongside her parents, reading books and wishing someone else would make the first move.

It was only after Teafin had manifested that Cedar had

reached out. Maybe she had seen something of herself in Fin—a girl who had stumbled into magic.

"Okay," said Fin, "I get it. But I mean—what about when you leave Aldermere? Magic fades outside of town. Couldn't you have stayed out of town for a few weeks and the bridge's magic would wear off?"

"The longest my family goes on vacation is for a few days, a week at most," replied Cedar. "For Christmas or my abuelita's birthday, we visit my dad's family. My mom's family isn't as close. And . . ." Her fingers tightened on her own arms. "Part of me likes the magic. Penny is a little weird and scary sometimes, but she's also funny and always there. If she was gone . . ." Cedar took a deep breath, then another. "I'd be alone."

"Well, what are we going to do now?" asked Fin. Someone had to say it. "River saw Brie."

"Of all the people to find out about Brie," said Eddie, "why'd it have to be him?"

"At least it wasn't SNACC," said Cedar. She looked relieved by the change of subject. "We'll have to move her. Now that Scott's caught a glimpse, he may come back."

"Where?" asked Eddie. "It's not like we've got a long list of places to stash a baby bigfoot."

They all looked at Brie. She was happily grooming her

whiskers, running her paws over her ears and cheeks. When she realized everyone was staring at her, she said, *"Meep?"*

"It's getting too late to look for her family today," said Cedar. "We'll have to try again tomorrow."

"But where do we keep her tonight?" said Eddie.

Fin gazed at the bigfoot. Her mind conjured up possibilities and almost immediately discarded them: the inn was full of people; the garage was too close to the street; Nick's house wouldn't work; the campsite wasn't safe. If the tea shop had still been around, she might have proposed bringing Brie there—after all, magical defenses would be a good way to keep the bigfoot safe. But the tea shop was gone, and—

A thought occurred to her. It was like unraveling a thread: the memory of the tea shop, her tea doppelgänger, all the chaos of last fall. . . .

She had found a place that was isolated. One where no one could find a secret.

"I think I know a spot," said Fin.

Scattered throughout Aldermere were water towers.

The town had no central water supply. When Aldermere was founded, a few enterprising individuals had constructed towers to collect the rain. But as years of drought crept across California, the towers were mostly replaced by well systems and tanks, with water occasionally delivered from out of town. Aunt Myrtle had a deep well that supplied both the cottage and the big house, and they'd been lucky it had never run dry.

Several of the old towers had been converted into other things: residences, storage, and even a few short-term rentals. The tourists who scoffed at the modern comforts of the inn could pay a little extra to walk up winding stairs and stay a few nights in a converted tower.

And there was one tower that had been abandoned.

Fin had visited it last fall, when she'd stepped through an unlabeled door. She had found herself on the north side of town, in a tower that had been mostly converted into a residence. It was lost to the woods, the undergrowth having crept right up to the foundation. Moss grew on the wooden ladder, and a cobweb shone in the afternoon light.

"I know this place," said Cedar. She and Fin had come to investigate, leaving Eddie back at the campsite with Brie. She touched the ladder, her fingers lingering on the old redwood. "We accidentally ended up here last fall."

Fin nodded. "I've come by a few times since then. No one's ever here."

Cedar's eyes shone with understanding. "Think it will work?"

"It's out of the way," said Fin. "It's high enough off the ground that hopefully even if a tourist walked by, Brie might not smell them."

Cedar tilted her head, hearing all the things that Fin did not say. "I thought you were afraid of heights."

"I'm not afraid of heights," said Fin. "I have a healthy respect for gravity."

That got her a smile, before Cedar's gaze darted away. She seemed unwilling or unable to hold Fin's eyes for more than a second.

Fin was tempted to pretend she hadn't noticed. To let things slide away. It might even have been a kindness, to allow Cedar the space she needed to process the last few hours. But Fin had retreated into silence many times before, and she knew the cost: secrets and unsaid things.

"Were you ever going to tell me?" she asked. "I mean, I get not telling your parents. And Eddie's a little intimidating sometimes because he's so . . ." She tried to search for the right word.

"Well-adjusted?" supplied Cedar.

"Yeah, that's it." Fin shoved her hands into the pockets of her jeans so she wouldn't fidget. "But you know how

I've messed things up, how I'm anxious and weird a lot of the time. If I said or did something to make you think you couldn't trust me—"

"No," said Cedar, her eyes flashing up to meet Fin's. "It wasn't about not trusting you. It was about . . . I mean, how do you tell someone something like that? That a cursed bridge gave me a shadow monster for a friend? That unless a person believes in magic, they can never know me? It's weird, even for Aldermere."

"I mean, it's no weirder than a baby bigfoot named after cheese," said Fin. "Or ten-legged mice or those deer with the weird shadows . . . hey, do you think they crossed the bridge too? Maybe that's why the deer around here all have creepy shadows."

"I don't think deer want things," said Cedar.

"Oh, I do," said Fin. "I once saw a deer staring at the apple tree in the Madeiras' yard like it wished it could climb."

Cedar laughed. "I do like her. Penny, I mean. She brings me things sometimes. I'll wake up and find stuff on my pillow like flowers and lost change and once even a shirt I saw in the inn lost and found that I wanted."

Realization went off at the back of Fin's mind like a small shock. She dug into her coat pocket and came up with the stolen locket. "I think this was meant for you, then."

Cedar frowned at the silver locket. "I . . . don't think so. I've never seen that before."

"I saw it at the Foragers' Market," said Fin. "And it was on my pillow last night after I spied on the SNACC Pack."

Cedar touched a finger to her lips. "Oh. Penny was loose for part of yesterday, when you and Eddie were hiking. I think she likes following you around. Maybe she saw you admiring the locket and went back for it."

"Why would a shadow like following me around?" asked Fin, bewildered.

Cedar shrugged, her eyes downcast. "Because I do." She looked tired and a little scared, like she was still expecting Fin to run at any moment.

That stopped Fin up short. She felt like a jerk for being so insensitive. "I like hanging out with you too. Besides Eddie, you're the first real friend I've ever had. And half the time I'm not sure he counts, because he's family. And he considers snakes and spiders to be his friends."

"He should have come to investigate the tower, then," said Cedar. "I'm sure we'll find at least a few spiders up there."

They climbed the ladder one at a time, taking each rung slowly. Fin tested her weight before putting each foot down, pulling herself higher and higher. The tower was about forty feet up, and whoever had owned it hadn't put in the effort to build stairs when they remodeled it into a house.

But then again, Fin wasn't sure it qualified as a house.

The door was labeled—NORTH WATER TOWER—but remained unlocked. Fin pushed it open and gazed into the dark interior. A few windows had been cut into the sides, and afternoon sunlight illuminated the space. There was a cot in the corner, a few rusted pieces of metal that might have been a camper's stove, a card table and two chairs, and a scattering of personal belongings like books and an old crate. The air was lit up with dust motes, and every surface looked soft with age and cobwebs. No one had been here in a long time—maybe not even since Fin and Cedar had been magicked inside. The floor was made of unvarnished redwood, and old tin-can lids had been used to fill in the knotholes. Fin made a mental note not to walk around barefoot.

"Well," said Cedar, touching one dusty wall, "I don't think anyone's going to look for a bigfoot here."

"I wonder if she'll be lonely at night," said Fin. "Maybe one of us should stay with her."

The thought didn't sit well with Fin; she had never snuck out. But she also knew that some dogs would whine and scratch at the door when they were left alone for too long.

Fin glanced at Cedar. She was pushing open a window,

trying to air out the tower. "You think you could get Penny to hang out with her?"

Cedar's fingers slipped on the window. "What?"

"Penny," said Fin. "She could keep an eye on Brie, right? And then none of us would have to sneak out."

Cedar crossed her arms over her stomach. "I don't know."

"I mean, you said she likes to run around while you sleep, right?" Fin waved, trying to encompass the whole of the tower in the gesture. "Could you tell her to come here?"

"She doesn't take orders," said Cedar. "I've tried a few times, but she just stares at me."

"Sounds like someone else I know," muttered Fin, thinking of the last time she'd tried to teach Morri to play fetch.

"If she listened to me, do you think she would have hurt Scott?" Cedar pointed out.

Fin shrugged. "I mean, he was being cruel to you when . . ." Her voice drifted off. A thought had occurred to her. "Hey, you remember Teafin?"

"Your made-of-tea doppelgänger?" Cedar sounded wry. "Yes, I do remember."

"She was also made of all the memories I tried to forget," said Fin. "She was my fear—and my anger. What if Penny is a little like that?"

"I never used magical tea, though," said Cedar. "I've never tried to change myself."

"Really?" said Fin. "So every time a tourist is rude to you when you're working at the coffee shop, your first instinct is to smile and pretend it doesn't matter?"

Surprise flashed across Cedar's face.

"I mean, I'm only around part of the time," said Fin, "and I've seen how some people treat you. You don't get mad, Cedar. Even when people are rude. When River kept forgetting your name, you made excuses for him."

"Well, that wasn't his fault," Cedar said quietly.

"He called you a freak," said Fin, "and that's when Penny hit him."

A frown line formed between Cedar's brows. "You think I wanted to cut Scott's hand?"

Fin shook her head. "No, I mean, I know you're not the kind of person to hurt someone. But in that moment, you were angry, right?"

Cedar looked as though she wanted to protest, but she nodded once.

"So Penny lashed out," said Fin. "We all—I mean, most of us, I think—feel things we'd rather not. My counselor says it's not the emotion that matters, but how we handle it. You do things for people all the time. You helped me last fall, and we were barely friends. You're kind to everyone, no matter how rude they are. But tell me . . . is it because you're actually that nice? Or because you're afraid people won't like you if you're not?"

That stumped Cedar. She looked down at her own shadow.

"I—I don't know," she said softly.

They stood there in silence. A few months ago, Fin knew, she would never have been brave enough to utter those words. But some things could not remain unsaid, not if a person truly cared about another. And Fin did care. She understood what it was to let fear drive her every action, and perhaps that was what let her see how Cedar's loneliness had shaped her.

"I think Penny's your loneliness," said Fin. "I think maybe the bridge took it, made it into something you could call your friend."

Cedar spread her fingers, twisting them so that the shadow she cast moved with her. "I was lonely for a long time," she admitted quietly. "I thought once I made friends, it'd be better. But now I have them, I'm scared of losing them."

"So you try and make yourself someone who doesn't care about that," said Fin. "You pretend so hard you almost believe it yourself."

Cedar looked at her sharply.

"It's what I did," said Fin. "And I do like being alone sometimes. For reading and just . . . thinking. But the only way you stop feeling lonely is to open up. To tell the truth, even when it's scary. Especially when it's scary."

"Is that what worked for you?"

"Yeah," said Fin.

Cedar swallowed. "I don't have any dark secrets," she said. "Mostly I . . . I worry that there is something wrong with me. Maybe it's not the bridge that made no one want to know me."

"Are you kidding?" said Fin. "You're not forgettable and there's nothing wrong with you. The first time we met, I asked for your name—you know how many people I did that with? Almost none. Even if I did forget it immediately, I still *wanted* to know you, even back then."

A small smile dawned on Cedar's face. "Really?"

"Really," said Fin. She looked around the dark and dusty water tower. "And I'm glad I do know you, because who else has a superpowered shadow horse that can help save a baby bigfoot?"

"Well," said Cedar, "when you say it like that . . ." She grinned, but it faded into a thoughtful glance around the water tower. She walked around the room's perimeter, touching the edges of the windows and running a hand over the old table. "I think you're right about keeping Brie here. It's out of the way. And maybe we should try to work with Penny. If I can get her to understand that I want to protect Brie, maybe she will too."

"I mean," said Fin, "it's not any less weird than most of our plans."

THIRTEEN
Training a Shadow

After they left the water tower, Cedar and Fin went their separate ways. Cedar needed to stop by the coffee shop and check in with her parents. Fin headed for the Ack. If she was going to smuggle a monster into an old, abandoned water tower, she needed supplies.

Aldermere had one general store. Aldermere Grocery & Tackle—the sign read ALDERMERE GROCERY & ACK, as some of the letters had rusted away—sold everything from groceries to fishing equipment to postcards. Once a week, Fin helped deliver items for the store. Between the magic and the ravens, mail had a tendency to go astray in Aldermere, and Mr. Hardin often ordered specialty items for locals. He had offered Fin and her mother store credit in exchange for her help. It gave Fin a sense of purpose, of belonging, and people tipped her with everything from home-baked goods to dollars to a note that read *Return in time of need*. The latter, given to her by the Reyes twins when Fin delivered a package to their home, was still tucked into Fin's sock drawer.

The Ack had the look of an old Western film, with a porch built of reclaimed redwood. A cat sat at the edge of the porch, his gaze fixated on something Fin couldn't see. His tail lashed back and forth.

Mr. Hardin was pouring something into tiny sachets when Fin walked inside. It smelled overpoweringly of lemon and something Fin couldn't quite identify. "What is that?" she asked curiously.

"Lemongrass," said Mr. Hardin, "peppermint, and a few other herbs." He had a pleasantly soft voice with a faint trace of a British accent.

"Is that a new air freshener?" said Fin. "It smells good."

"It's for the whintossers," said Mr. Hardin. "I think there's a new colony under the porch. The blasted things ate the roots from the irises I just planted, and now the cat's trying to hunt them. The whintossers, not the irises. I don't want an infestation while that film crew is running around.

I'll put these under the porch." He picked up one sachet. It was about the size of Fin's fist. "Whintossers don't like them because the smell overpowers everything else. So they'll leg it back to their burrows."

The whintossers were among the more common cryptids of Aldermere: shy, tiny rodents with about eight or ten legs and a tendency to steal crumbs and to nibble at gardens. They were fuzzy and cute—and altogether unsettling when they walked like a spider.

"You here for deliveries?" Mr. Hardin asked as he knotted another sachet closed. He leaned on the counter. "You're a day early."

Fin could barely remember what day of the week it was—between spring break, Brie, the SNACC Pack, River, and now Cedar's shadow, time had taken on a meaningless quality. "No," she said. "Actually, I need to grab some food."

"Well, you know where to find that," said Mr. Hardin, giving her another smile before picking up an empty sachet.

Usually it was Mom who did their shopping, but if they were going to smuggle a bigfoot across town, Fin knew they were going to need snacks. The Ack didn't have a huge selection; it mostly stocked the basics, with a few nods to the hikers and campers. There were bags of marshmallows and chocolate bars right next to the trail mix and jerky. Fin passed those by and picked up a loaf of bread, a cabbage, and a bit of cheddar cheese—just in case they needed a treat.

Mr. Hardin rang her up using her mom's account. He also slid one of Fin's favorite candy bars into the bag before she could protest. "Free of charge. I'll see you tomorrow," he said handing over the paper bag.

Fin nodded and turned away—then she froze.

Nick had said that bigfoots could tell if a person was a child or an adult by *smelling* them.

Fin whirled around, facing the counter. "Mr. Hardin, can I buy one of those sachets?"

His graying brows swept up into his hair. "You having trouble with the whintossers too?" he asked.

"Frank just gave my mom some new rhododendrons," said Fin, because that wasn't a lie.

He picked up a sachet and tossed it to her. "You can have one."

She fumbled the catch, but she quickly picked it up and shoved it into her pocket. At once, the smell of lemon and mint enveloped her. She could no longer smell the familiar scents of the store: old wood, various foods, and an undercurrent of leather. That was good—if Fin couldn't smell anything, maybe Brie wouldn't either. "Thanks," she said gratefully. "See you tomorrow."

Fin trotted home, keeping her gaze averted from tourists and locals alike. She didn't have time to stop for a chat. Finally she rounded the corner and saw the big house. Her shoulders slumped in relief, and she hastened her pace.

When she returned to their small campsite, Eddie was sitting on the old log and Brie was playing with a teddy bear.

"Where did you find that?" asked Fin, setting down her bag of supplies. Eddie looked over his shoulder at her, grinning. "Found it in a corner of my closet. It's old, and I don't mind if it gets a little torn up. And look at her—she's having fun."

Brie was tossing the teddy bear into the air, then running in circles around where it fell, before picking it up and snuggling it. Then she tossed it again.

It was adorable.

"Where's Cedar?" asked Eddie.

"Off to make sure her parents don't think she's avoiding them or anything," said Fin. She sat next to him, leaning on her knees. She couldn't quite believe it had only been this morning they'd been eating cinnamon buns and walking through the forest in search of a bigfoot herd.

"I think we should move her soon," said Fin. "Before Mom comes home. The water tower was still empty, and I think we can get her there without her panicking." She slid the sachet from her pocket. "If we put this nearby, she won't be able to smell any adults."

Eddie wrinkled his nose at the overpowering scent. "Okay, that's what the smell was. I thought maybe you had a new soap or something."

"As if I had time to shower," said Fin, with a small roll of her eyes. "As if there's time for anything but figuring out what to do with her."

Brie looked up and meeped a greeting at Fin.

Eddie rose from the log, brushing rotted wood from his jeans. "How are we going to do this? Shove her in a backpack? Steal Mrs. Brackenbury's dog stroller?"

"There's a wheelbarrow in the garage," said Fin. "I saw it last time your mom sent me in there. We can toss a blanket over the top so no one will see her."

"You think she'll put up with that?" Eddie slid a skeptical glance toward Brie.

Fin reached down into the paper bag and withdrew the loaf of bread, the cabbage, and the cheese. "I think we'll make it worth her while."

Which was how Fin found herself in front of a rusting blue wheelbarrow, telling Eddie where to avoid potholes, cracks in the pavement, and the occasional stray root. They had tossed a quilt over the wheelbarrow, and the scent of the sachet was overpowering. Eddie grunted, sweat beading at his brow as he pushed the wheelbarrow down the street.

"I told you," Eddie said through gritted teeth, "that you should've gotten a little red wagon for your deliveries. Imagine how much easier this would've been."

A few ravens croaked from a tree overhead. Fin had the distinct impression they were laughing at the two humans.

"Well, give me a turn," said Fin. "If you're getting tired."

The wheelbarrow hit a bump, and there was a small, indignant squeak from beneath the blanket. Fin pulled it up at one corner. Inside, Brie had crumbs of cheddar cheese on her whiskers and a confused look on her face. "We're almost there," said Fin, in what she hoped was a soothing voice.

Brie meeped and went back to devouring a slice of bread.

Fin dropped the blanket back in place.

"If we had bicycles with baskets . . ." said Eddie longingly.

"We couldn't ride them up this path." Fin reached down, grabbed the lip of the wheelbarrow, and helped haul it over another protruding root.

The journey felt like a long one—full of grunting, sweaty

T-shirts, and pounding hearts. Fin was sure that they'd see a tourist around every corner, that a random hiker would want to know what two kids were pushing in a very old wheelbarrow, that someone would know, someone would see, and everything would come crashing down.

The path twined up a small hill, leading to the tower. Eddie heaved the wheelbarrow to a halt, panting as he leaned against a tree. Fin peeled back the blanket and found Brie gazing up at her. The bigfoot still looked a little confused by the journey, but at least she wasn't frightened. She meeped a greeting, and Fin placed her on the ground. Brie began sniffing at a fern frond.

"I knew this tower was here," said Eddie, "but I thought someone lived in it." He held up one hand against a shaft of afternoon sunlight, shielding his eyes as he gazed at the water tower.

"It's always been empty when I've come here," said Fin. "It could be someone's vacation spot, but they haven't been back in months. Maybe they live out of state."

"Mom would know." Eddie let his hand fall back to his side. "I'll ask her when she comes back. She knows everyone in town." He glanced around. "At least we're away from the hiking trails. No one's probably going to come too close to this place."

True enough. There was an old NO TRESPASSING sign rusting on a nearby tree.

Fin reached down and picked up the sachet she'd placed in the wheelbarrow. "We should put this in the tower with her." Fin tucked the sachet into her pocket, where she'd also put the locket and the notes Nick had given her. She was carrying around a lot these days.

Eddie went to scout the area, appeasing his curiosity while Fin waved a fern frond at Brie. The bigfoot was a little sleepy after her meal of cheese and bread, and her attempts to catch the fern were half-hearted. She yawned, her whiskers pressing against her cheeks. She really was lovable, Fin thought, with a rush of fondness. She'd never had a pet—and Brie wasn't a pet, she reminded herself—but Fin thought it must be something like this.

Cedar appeared after ten minutes. "Oh, good," she said, walking over to Fin. "You managed to get her here. Sorry I wasn't able to help—my dad needed another pair of hands in the coffee shop. There was a rush of road trippers who needed buckets of caffeine."

"We managed," said Fin. She nodded at the wheelbarrow. "Carried her here in that. And blocked out her sense of smell with this." She plucked the sachet out of her pocket and held it up. "Got the idea from Mr. Hardin trying to get rid of his whintosser invasion."

Cedar smiled, sitting down beside Fin and Brie. The bigfoot gave her a sleepy blink. "I saw the SNACC Pack on the way here. They were filming a scene outside the Ack. Probably because it's got that old Western look."

Fin wrinkled her nose. "I wonder what Mr. Hardin thinks about that."

"I don't know, but Dad still won't give them the Wi-Fi password," said Cedar, with a sly little smile. "I heard them complaining that no one in town will—except for the inn, of course."

"Well, maybe that will make them leave faster," said Fin.

Eddie tromped into sight, kicking a little mud from his boots. He had a bit of moss dangling from one sleeve and dried redwood needles in his hair. "Hey," he said, seeing Cedar. "Glad you could make it. I've never explored around here. Caught sight of a cool-looking lizard, but I couldn't catch it."

"Trying to find Brie a roommate?" asked Cedar.

Eddie laughed. "I'm not sure a lizard would enjoy being tossed around like that teddy bear."

"Speaking of," said Fin, with a significant look at Cedar. "You want to try summoning Penny?"

A flicker of unease crossed Cedar's face. She took a

breath and lowered herself to the ground, as though she was bracing herself to pick up something heavy. She touched a finger to her own shadow. When she straightened, a tendril of darkness followed that finger. For a heartbeat, it looked as delicate and sticky as a cobweb. Its edges solidified until that monstrous horse stood before them.

"Hey, Penny," said Cedar softly.

The horse looked at Cedar with its eyeless face.

Eddie and Fin kept a careful distance, but Brie was fascinated. She walked closer, her tiny paws pressed against her chest and whiskers pointed forward. Fin made a sound in her throat—she wasn't sure if she was going to warn Brie or say something to Cedar—but then Penny took a step forward. The horse snuffled Brie for a few moments before blowing out a gusty breath.

Fin didn't know how shadows could breathe, never mind let out a huff. But at least the noise was one of acceptance; Penny nudged Brie in a way that looked friendly.

Brie reached out with her tiny paws and began grasping at the dark tendrils of Penny's mane, as if she wanted to climb the horse. "Oh no," said Cedar, reaching down to pick up Brie. The bigfoot made a sad-sounding *meep* as she was handed off to Eddie.

"Have you ever tried to ride her?" asked Fin. Emboldened

by Brie's interaction with Penny, Fin took a step forward and extended her fingers to the horse. Penny sniffed, then nudged her nose into Fin's palm. Obligingly, Fin stroked the shadow's nose.

"Once," said Cedar. "When I was, like, nine."

"And how'd it go?" asked Eddie eagerly. He sat down beside Brie, waving the teddy bear so she'd be occupied.

Cedar grimaced. "You remember that video that went viral a few years back? The one with the kid who tried to ride a sheep and the sheep bolted and the kid went flying? And how everyone kept setting it to different music clips?"

Eddie nodded.

"It was like that," said Cedar. "Only without the soundtrack."

Fin laughed, unable to help herself. "Why don't we try something easier?" she said.

Cedar glanced at her. "Like what?"

Fin shrugged. "I've been teaching Morri to play fetch."

"You want to play fetch with a shadow horse?" said Eddie.

Fin picked up a fallen stick. "I think we should start small." She handed it to Cedar. "She's yours. You should try."

Cedar took the stick, eyeing it with a certain amount of skepticism. Then she held it out before Penny. "Hey," she said softly, her voice little more than a murmur. "You want to play a game?"

Penny sniffed the stick, then shook her head. Her mane whipped a little and Fin retreated, remembering how one of those threads had sliced at River's hand.

Cedar pulled her arm back and tossed the stick. It flew, end over end, into a clump of ferns.

Penny watched the stick as it fell. Then she looked at Cedar.

Fin and Eddie did not laugh. But it was only through sheer force of will.

"Good try," said Eddie, his amusement bleeding into every word.

"Hey, we all start somewhere," said Fin. "And Morri still won't fetch on command. She just shows up with spare keys and change."

Cedar smiled. "Where is your raven?"

"I'm pretty sure she's not my raven," said Fin. "I'm her human." Her gaze swept up toward the redwoods. There were no ravens in sight, but she could hear the distant croaks of a nearby unkindness. "Last time I saw her, she was following SNACC. Maybe she still is. Or maybe she's off digging for food in someone's garbage."

"Equal priorities for a raven," said Cedar gravely, before a grin tugged at her mouth. She reached down for another stick. "Let's try this again." She waved the stick in front of Penny and tossed it into the ferns.

Fin wasn't sure how something without eyes could give someone a flat stare, but Penny managed.

"If Penny is connected to your emotions," said Fin, "maybe you have to want to get the stick? And she'll feel it?"

Cedar's mouth scrunched to one side. She regarded her monster, then closed her eyes and took a deep breath. "I want the stick," she murmured. "I want the stick."

Penny shifted on her hooves but made no move toward the stick.

"*Do* you want the stick?" asked Eddie curiously.

Cedar opened her eyes. "Not really."

"That solves it, then," said Eddie. "Mom always says it's easier to lie out loud than to yourself."

"Well, what's your plan?" Fin turned toward Eddie.

Eddie picked up the teddy bear and tossed it to Brie. She caught it and threw it into the air before rolling around on the ground, wrestling fiercely with the toy. "I don't know," he said. "What's something she brought to you in the past?"

Cedar's brows pulled together. "Flowers that I liked. She

ripped them out by the roots. Our poor neighbors thought the whintossers did it."

"And this," said Fin. She dug into her pocket and pulled out the silver locket. It swung between her fingers. "We think she stole this from the Foragers' Market for me." She sighed. "I should probably find a way to give it back."

Eddie frowned. "Why not throw that into the woods? See if Penny will fetch it?"

A squirm of panic went through Fin's stomach. "What if we don't find it again?"

"Sticks aren't cutting it," said Eddie. He gazed intently at the locket, then at Penny. "But if she's connected to Cedar's emotions, why is she bringing you gifts?"

Cedar blew out an impatient breath. "Probably because I'm terrified of losing the only friends I have," she said with startling honesty. "And being nice and giving people things are the only ways I know how to cling on to them." She shot Fin a look, silencing her. "And before you say anything, I know this is a me problem, not a you problem. You're not the kind of person to abandon people. It's part of the reason I wanted to be your friend."

Eddie tapped a finger against his chin. "Okay, that's it, then. Penny finds a locket to bribe Fin into being your friend." He wrinkled his nose. "Hey, why isn't the monster horse bringing me gifts? Should I be offended?"

At that, Penny lifted her head and glanced at Eddie. Fin wasn't sure if it was because the horse understood his words or because it felt the echo of Cedar's emotions. But before anyone could say a word, the horse tore off into the woods. She moved silently as a shadow, fluidly as spilled ink.

For a heartbeat, all was still. Fin found herself holding her breath, listening for any sound in the woods. Even Brie froze, her paws clutching the teddy bear. She lifted her nose, whiskers pointed forward, sniffing the air.

Penny reappeared, flowing up through the shadows of the woods, rising like a swimmer from water. She trotted to Eddie, lowering her head. And then she opened her mouth and spat something into his lap.

A lizard. It fell onto Eddie's knee, clinging to his jeans. It blinked a few times, looking confused but unhurt.

Penny took two steps back. She stared at Eddie expectantly.

Eddie slowly reached down and held the lizard. It crawled up his fingers, holding on for dear life. "Oh," said Eddie. "I . . . uh. Thanks?"

A startled laugh burst from Fin. She couldn't help herself—it was too weird *not* to be funny. Eddie joined in a moment later, laughing as the lizard scurried down his wrist, gave Penny a wary glance, then ran into the bushes. Even Cedar was grinning ruefully, her hand pressed to her mouth.

"So Fin gets a locket and I get a lizard," said Eddie, once he'd recovered enough to speak.

"Well, that fits." Fin shook her head, still laughing.

An hour later, the sun was beginning to ebb from the sky and Penny hadn't fetched a single stick. But nor did she seem inclined to hurt anyone or vandalize a garden. Finally the horse bent down and melted back into Cedar's normal shadow.

Brie had fallen asleep in Eddie's lap after devouring another slice of bread. He slung her over his shoulder, and climbed the ladder to the water tower. They left her with a bowl of water, several apples, a few more slices of bread, and the teddy bear for company. Even so, Fin kept looking at where Brie was curled up on an old rug. She didn't want Brie to think she'd been abandoned. "What if she gets lonely?"asked Fin.

Eddie shrugged. "I don't think we have a choice, not unless one of us sneaks out tonight."

Cedar let out a breath. "I'm sorry, but I'm not sure I can tell Penny to stay here. I mean, I can tell her, but she isn't all that excited about listening to me today." She flicked an irritated look at her own shadow, which looked resolutely human.

"Well," said Fin. "Maybe we should draw straws?"

"I'll do it," said Eddie.

Of course he would. Because Eddie was fearless and cared more about animals than anyone she'd ever met. But he couldn't. "No," said Fin. "If you sneak out with Aunt Myrtle gone, Mom will never let you stay over again. It's part of the whole mom club thing. She would blame herself."

"I could . . ." Cedar began to say, but Fin shook her head.

"I'll do it," said Fin. "Like you said, I'm in charge. Sort of. And, well—Nick did entrust this mission to me. I won't make either of you do this."

"We could go together," said Eddie.

"Someone has to pretend we're still there, if Mom checks." Fin glanced up at the sky. The sun was falling behind the trees, descending toward the horizon. "We should get back soon."

"I can stay with Brie until sunset," said Cedar. "That way she won't be left alone for too long."

Fin nodded. "And tomorrow," she said, trying to infuse her words with certainty, "we'll go back out and find her family."

FOURTEEN

Interlude with a Raven

Her name had not always been Morrigan.

It had once been something wordless, a croon in her mother's chest. An unsaid thing. But most humans did not understand the clicks and chatter of the ravens, so the one called Fin had given the raven a human name.

Morri.

The raven rather liked her name. It was soft, rounded in the humans' mouths. It sounded like small children begging their parents for more, more and then leaving crumbs scattered across the sidewalk. It was a good name. And her human was a good sort too. Not quite as good as a raven, but Fin gave her treats and neck scratches.

Ravens saw everything. They watched from tree branches, from power lines, from atop cars and houses. They listened, cocking their heads as humans chattered and cars backfired and dogs barked. And ravens gossiped among themselves, sharing news in croaks and burbles. They knew which humans had paid their weekly tithes and which hadn't. They knew when Mrs. Brackenbury took her dog for a walk and left crumbles of treats in her wake. They saw the young Carver girl trudging home with her hands shoved in her pockets and how a tourist bumped into her and didn't apologize. They knew when Mrs. Madeira wasn't having a good day, and sometimes the ravens would leave small trinkets at her windowsill. Mr. Madeira gave them scraps of bread from the inn.

Ravens knew the delicate balance of obligation.

And so Morri followed the film crew. Not because it had been asked of her, but because she could see how Fin worried. If her human did not trust these outsiders, Morri would ensure nothing they did went unnoticed.

She followed them to the inn, to the coffee shop, through the town.

They didn't notice her, of course. All ravens looked alike to them. So when two of the outsiders tromped down a southern trail, they did not lower their voices. They took samples of fur they found clinging to blackberry brambles—which Morri knew belonged to a raccoon that lived nearby.

"Hopefully I'll be able to upload these pictures when we get back." The human with the shiny lenses fiddled with his camera. "I can't believe it took a day to fix the Wi-Fi."

"Welcome to the wilderness, Michael." The woman threw out an arm, as if to encompass all the forest. "At least out here no one's glaring at us."

"You got that too?" said the young man with a small laugh. "Thought it was just me."

"I don't think this town is all that enthused about any of us," said the woman. "Which is stupid. I heard that town with the chupacabra had a huge jump in visitors after episode twenty-four went live."

"Yeah, but the mystery spot shut down," said Michael drily. "So I can see it from their perspective."

The woman snorted. "That's not our fault." She turned in a small circle, looking around at the trail. "All right, nature calls."

"Classy, Ana."

"Well, I'm not walking back to the hotel. Watch my stuff." Ana threw a grin at Michael, set her backpack on the ground, and made her way deeper into the forest, leaving the trail behind. Morri looked from human to human, wondering who to follow. The man was wholly absorbed by his equipment, which made him boring. Morri's gaze fell on Ana, decision made. The raven hopped from branch to branch as the woman tentatively pushed aside the undergrowth and angled herself between bushes.

Ana glanced back the way she'd come, as if to make sure Michael couldn't see her. Which meant she was not paying attention to where her feet were. Morri cocked her head as Ana stepped backward around a tree and then stumbled, her heel caught on a ridge. She bit back a cry as she tripped, falling onto her hands. It looked more surprising than painful. Irritation flashed across the woman's face, and she muttered a few insults to the forest. She pushed herself into a crouch, brushing the needles from her bare palms. She looked down to see what she had tripped over.

Morri heard her sharp intake of breath.

It had not been a stray stick or a root that had snagged the woman's heel.

The evening light cast long shadows across the huge footprint. Far larger than the ones that crisscrossed town.

It was the width of a garbage-bin lid and pressed three inches into the damp earth.

Morri watched as the human considered the sight before her.

"They must've made a bigger footprint mold," whispered Ana.

For a few moments Ana couldn't move. She reached out with shaky fingers, touched the indentations that looked like toes. Her breath quickened. She stepped out of the footprint, turning in a half circle. And that was when she saw the rest of them.

There were dozens of footprints, hidden beneath the fern fronds and softened by the bed of redwood needles. Enormous footprints trailed through the area, as if giants had patrolled the forest.

Far too many footprints for a single person—or even a few of them—to create with a mold.

"It's a prank, it's a stupid—" Ana's words snagged in her throat. She swallowed several times before she said, "Michael!" Her voice came out a little strangled as she turned toward the trail and hurried back.

Morri knew the creatures who made these tracks; they were the forestkind—those of the large feet and songs too soft for human ears. They wandered the old growth, avoiding the humankind as if their lives depended on it. Which it did.

Ravens were lucky, Morri knew. They could survive anywhere. But the forestkind were different. Their ability to blend into the forest, to avoid notice, was all that protected them. For a herd to come this close to the town was unheard of. But such was the love of parents looking for a lost young one.

Ana returned to the human called Michael, sputtering words like "footprints," and "prank." And while he went to investigate, Morri fluttered to the ground behind them. One of the human's lenses sat forgotten by his camera. Morri picked up the glittering thing in her beak. Spreading her wings, she took to the air.

She knew someone who wanted to find these creatures too.

FIFTEEN
Bigfoot Impossible

Fin had never snuck out of the cottage.

She'd never snuck out of *anywhere* before.

She knew how to do it in theory, of course. She'd seen movies where people opened a window and stepped outside—or if they were on a second story, effortlessly climbed down a conveniently placed tree. The problem with escaping the cottage was that the floorboards had a tendency to squeak, Mom was a light sleeper, and there were no trees close enough to Fin's window to descend. And even if there were, redwoods didn't make for easy climbing.

"This is never going to work," she muttered, peering

through her window. It wasn't that much of a drop, but the incline of the A-frame roof looked intimidating.

"It's gonna work," said Eddie.

"How do you know?"

"Because if it doesn't work, then I've spent the last hour practicing this for nothing," said Eddie, holding up his work.

It had been Eddie's idea to raid the garage for a piece of old rope. It was plastic, left over from the days when Aunt Myrtle had hung a swing near the garage. Eddie had been tying knots in the rope for the last hour, claiming that handholds would make it easier to climb down.

"You do realize if this goes wrong, I'm probably going to end up grounded," said Fin. "And you're going to have to work with Cedar and her very unreliable shadow monster to get Brie back to her family."

"As long as we have a plan." Eddie flashed her a smile.

Mom had come home carrying boxes of pot roast and vegetables, and a coconut cake for dessert. The three of them ate at the table, talking about how their sleeping in the woods had gone. Fin left the details vague, but she did mention their midnight raven visitor—without mentioning her own excursion into the woods. When Mom inquired about the two tents, Fin had said, "I'll take them down tomorrow."

"Good," said Mom, picking up a forkful of potato. "I

don't want Myrtle coming back to find her tents destroyed by the deer."

"Deer don't destroy tents," Eddie had replied. "They will try to look for snacks around them, though. Which we didn't leave behind," he added hastily, sensing Mom's disapproval in the silence. "That would be stupid! Because bears!"

After dinner, Fin and Eddie retreated to the loft. Eddie reluctantly worked on his book report while Fin fidgeted with her stolen locket. She wound the chain around her fingers again and again, her stomach as knotted as the rope. The minutes dragged. Fin kept thinking of Brie escaping from the tower, or someone finding her, and all the other things that could go awry. Her mind wouldn't settle, no matter how many times she tried to do a breathing exercise or told herself that there was no point in worrying about things that might never come to pass.

Finally, around nine, the quiet drone of a fan came from Mom's room. After years of sleeping in cities, Mom liked a little white noise while she slept. Fin waited another fifteen or so minutes before she deemed it safe. "All right," she said. She wore her heavy army surplus coat, boots, and a backpack slung over her shoulders. "Ready?"

Eddie gave her a thumbs-up. "Ready for Bigfoot Impossible."

"Of course you're ready," said Fin. "You get to watch."

Eddie had tied the rope around one of the wooden banisters that cordoned off the loft's steep edge. He gave it a hard tug, then nodded in satisfaction. "It's good."

Fin took a breath. She wasn't scared of heights, not precisely. But when she opened the window and peered down, her stomach swooped.

"I've got this," she whispered. "I've got this."

She let the rope fall—it was thin, but the corded plastic had been strong enough to hold up a swing for many years. It would hold her. And the slope of the roof wasn't so steep.

The hardest part was stepping off the windowsill. Her sweaty fingers slid along the rope, and she took a sharp, unsteady breath. Her whole body was wound tight as a rubber band about to snap. She turned so that her back was to the dark woods and tried to ease herself through the window. Eddie watched, his face serious but not overly concerned. He wasn't scared, Fin told herself, so she wouldn't be either.

And besides, Brie was worth this.

Fin stepped onto the slope of the roof, crouching at an angle. She was reminded of that video of Ana Bell in a mystery spot, having to lean to keep her balance in a crooked house. Her fingers snagged on one of the knots and she swallowed, grateful for Eddie's handiwork. Each knot was a small handhold, making it easier for her to half shuffle, half walk her way down the roof. Her boots found purchase on the rough asphalt shingles as she descended.

It seemed to take an hour to creep down, but it was probably more like a minute. Her knuckles ached, her fingers were red with effort, and every inch felt like a small victory. One small shuffle, one knot downward.

Then her feet hit the edge of the roof and she finally allowed herself to look down. It was perhaps a four-foot drop, and she forced herself not to hesitate. If she hesitated, she wasn't sure she could pry her fingers from the rope.

Fin dropped. She hit the ground on both feet, the impact jolting up through her knees.

But she was on the ground. And the rope was still dangling out the window, with Eddie beaming down at her.

"That was awesome," he said gleefully.

Fin pressed a finger to her mouth. The last thing she needed was for Mom to wake up. Eddie covered his laugh with a hand, then gave her a wave.

"See you in the morning," she whispered.

There was a flashlight in her backpack, but she didn't dare turn it on. Not yet. She jogged past the big house, down the street, and toward the woods. She navigated the darkness by the light that spilled through neighbors' windows. Aldermere did not have street lamps, and the one time Mayor Downer proposed them, she had been outvoted. Finally, Fin stepped from the pavement onto the dirt path and twisted her flashlight to life.

Her heart throbbed in her chest; she was keenly aware of how she did not belong in the forest. Not at night. Not alone. Nighttime was for monsters. Everyone knew that. It was why kids shut their closets at night, why they invoked the power of blankets and walls to protect them.

Fin forced herself to breathe more slowly. Perhaps if she could trick her lungs into thinking she was unafraid, the rest of her body would follow. She kept her pace steady, not quite a jog because one did not jog through a forest at night. The flashlight's beam bounced along the path, cheerful and bright.

And then Fin saw something from the corner of her eye.

A flicker of movement.

She whirled, the flashlight's beam falling into the undergrowth.

Fin couldn't have picked out many details; the creature vanished as the light fell upon it. But it couldn't have been human. The shape was all wrong.

Fin's heart began to race. Her first thought was that it

was a bear, but the creature had moved too quickly. A cougar, then? But—

Then something stepped from the woods and onto the path.

She sucked in a breath so quickly that it hurt, the air scraping her throat. She wanted to cry out, to run, to turn around and retreat back toward Aldermere and safety and home. Her shaking hands clutched at the flashlight, the illumination trembling as it was aimed at the path.

But when the light fell on the ground, nothing was there.

Fin stood there, adrenaline making her feel both too hot and too cold.

Something was circling her. But every time she looked directly at it, it flickered away. Like a creature that could only be looked at through the corner of her eye.

She could not retreat. The water tower was closer than town. If she could get there, she'd be safe. She could lock the door behind her, wait with Brie until morning came.

But she was frozen in place. Her feet would not move, no matter how many times Fin told them to.

She heard the crack of a twig behind her.

Fin's breathing stopped altogether. She was frozen with fear, ice in her veins, her skin clammy. Part of her whispered that she shouldn't turn around. In all the old myths and fairy tales, a person should never turn around. Nothing ever good lurked behind—and glancing over one's shoulder led to lovers being ripped back to the underworld, to monsters standing a hair's breadth behind them, to unseen things becoming all too real.

But the need to know was too great.

Fin turned as slowly as she could and looked over her shoulder. The flashlight stayed pointing ahead, the light wavering in her unsteady hands.

And she saw the hulking form of a monstrous horse standing behind her.

Fin let out a startled cry, stumbling to one side. The flashlight rolled from her hands, light falling uselessly on tree roots and wildflowers. Fin was on the ground, legs tangled and breath heaving. There was just enough light to see Penny standing beside her.

"You," said Fin, torn between relief and anger. "What are you doing here?"

Penny shook her head. She stepped forward and nudged the flashlight so that the light was angled away from her. And then Fin understood.

No wonder Fin hadn't seen the shadow horse. She'd been turning the flashlight on her—which couldn't be healthy for a shadow. Fin wondered if the concentrated light hurt her. "Sorry," said Fin. "I—I didn't realize it was you. Is Cedar here?"

Penny gave her an eyeless stare. It was rather unnerving. But Fin remembered what Cedar had said—that Penny roamed the woods when Cedar was dreaming.

"You want to come along?" said Fin.

Penny bobbed her head.

"All right," said Fin. She picked up the flashlight, taking care to angle it away from Penny as she walked toward the water tower. The horse fell into step beside Fin's shadow rather than Fin herself. Perhaps that was how a shadow navigated the world, Fin thought. Maybe Penny saw the dark places, the little echoes people made without noticing.

Fin turned a corner and saw the water tower. A relieved sigh escaped her. Nothing was out of place. Fin clicked off the flashlight, shoving it in her coat pocket before climbing the ladder. She realized her mistake when she was halfway up.

Fin looked down. Penny stood on the ground, her tail flicking.

"Sorry, you can't climb, can you?" asked Fin. "You can stay down there, maybe? Watch out for bears and cougars? And anyone with a camera?"

Penny shifted her weight from one hoof to the other.

It looked like a restless gesture, but before Fin could say anything more, the shadow blurred. She melted into the ground, and then a dark smudge trailed up the ladder. Fin watched as darkness darted through the wooden rungs, slipping through her fingers and gliding upward. It felt like stepping into a strangely warm river, and she shuddered hard. A few heartbeats later, the shadow eased through the crack beneath the front door.

"Well," said Fin. "I guess you can." She hastily climbed the rest of the way into the tower.

Brie was awake, holding the teddy bear in her paws. Fin carefully clicked on the flashlight, setting it so the beam was angled toward the ceiling. The old furniture cast eerie shadows along the walls, but nothing was quite as eerie as the horse taking form a few feet from Brie. As Penny coalesced in a blur of darkness, Fin was reminded of a nature documentary she'd seen about squids vanishing into ink.

Brie meeped a greeting.

Penny leaned down and nudged the bigfoot. Brie squeaked and stroked the shadow horse's nose.

"Well," said Fin, plopping onto the floor. She settled her backpack between her legs and unzipped it. "I'm glad everyone's getting along."

Brie hurried toward Fin, nuzzling against her leg. For a

moment, it was very cute. And then Fin realized that Brie was trying to get at one of her pockets, looking for snacks. "You're worse than the cat at the Ack," said Fin, grinning. She pulled an apple from her backpack and tossed it to Brie. The bigfoot caught it and began devouring the snack with obvious delight.

"Makes sense," said Fin. "If you guys are herbivores, it must take a lot of food to keep a bigfoot going. And you're still growing. No wonder you're like a bottomless pit." She glanced at Penny. The horse was investigating the inside of the water tower: sniffing at the old chair, at the table, nudging at the walls.

Exhaustion settled into Fin's arms and legs, weighing her down. Between River's catching a glimpse of Brie, the revelations about the toll bridge and Penny, and the constant vigilance of looking out for the SNACC Pack, all Fin wanted was a few hours of rest and peace. She closed her eyes, listening to the crunching sounds of a bigfoot devouring an apple. It was strangely soothing.

And then someone knocked at the front door.

Fin fumbled her way upright, hurtling to the door. She grabbed the flashlight, heart pounding with fresh adrenaline. She opened it, expecting to see Cedar or Eddie. Or maybe even River.

A raven sat atop the ladder, looking expectant.

Morri.

Relief crashed through Fin. It was the raven. Once again, visiting her at night.

"You have got to stop doing that," she said.

Morri tried to croak, but it came out as a low grinding sound. There was something in her beak, Fin realized. Morri hopped into the tower, bouncing closer to Fin before setting something on the floor.

Fin picked it up. It was glass, rimmed with dark plastic. A camera lens. It looked new and expensive.

"Did you take this from the SNACC Pack?" said Fin, amused.

Morri tilted her head back and forth. Then she opened her beak and said, "Prank."

Fin fell over backward. The flashlight tumbled from her hand, its beam bouncing off one of the walls. Penny leaped to one side to avoid the falling illumination, then gave Fin what she could only call a reproachful eyeless look. Brie hurried forward to pick up the camera lens. She sniffed it, then began nibbling at the edge. "Oh no," said Fin, taking it from her. "That's not for eating." She turned toward Morri. The raven seemed confused by all the commotion.

"Did you talk?" said Fin.

Morri ruffled her feathers. "Footprints," she said, in that same voice. Feminine, but a little husky, and oddly familiar.

Ravens could imitate sounds; Fin had heard one raven perfectly croak out a car alarm. But it was one thing for the ravens to mimic car noises and clicks, and it was completely another to hear a very human-sounding voice emerging from Morri's beak. Like a deer suddenly opening its mouth and saying, "Hello."

It was unnerving, to say the least.

"Prank?" said Fin. "Did you say 'prank'?"

Morri puffed herself up. As if she thought Fin was very slow for not catching on immediately. "Prank," she said. "Footprints. Prank."

And then Fin realized where she'd heard that voice before. Ana Bell. That was Ana Bell's voice.

Prank. Footprints.

Fin's mind raced. "Did they find Brie's footprints?" she said.

Morri looked at her. It was a very flat, disappointed look.

Fin hadn't even realized that ravens could look disappointed until now. "Prank." Then she fluttered to Fin's arm and began nibbling at the camera lens.

Prank. A memory came back to her: Ana Bell speaking of the supposed prank up north in Bluff Creek. Of footprints even larger than the ones Brie had left scattered through town. Of logging equipment too heavy for a human to move, and unsolved mysteries.

And then she realized that Morri's imitation of Ana's voice had held a note that Fin had never heard before: *fear*.

Fin went very still. She wasn't sure what could make a person like Ana afraid, but she was pretty sure it would take more than a few shovel-sized footprints left in the dirt.

"The herd," breathed Fin. "Did the film crew find the herd?"

Morri blinked. "Footprints," she repeated.

Okay, Fin couldn't blame Morri for being irritated with her this time. "So SNACC didn't find the bigfoot herd," she said. "They found tracks. Can you take me there, tomorrow?"

Morri bobbed her head.

"Good," said Fin, relieved.

Morri looked expectant, so Fin dug into her backpack and came up with a slice of bread. She tore off a piece and tossed it to Morri, who accepted the reward as if it was her due.

Brie meeped loudly. This time it sounded indignant.

Fin tossed her a piece of bread. Then she looked at Penny. "I don't suppose you eat?"

Penny's head turned away.

"Good, because I'm running out of snacks." Fin crumpled the empty bag of bread into her pocket. Her mind was racing. Morri had been watching the SNACC Pack—and they had found more footprints. They wouldn't necessarily lead to Brie's family, but it was a start. Fin sat down on the floor again, tucking the lens away. She would tell the others tomorrow.

Fin looked at the bigfoot, the shadow monster, and the raven.

"And here I thought I might be lonely tonight," she said, pulling a blanket from her backpack.

SIXTEEN
Broken Ferns

It was before dawn when Fin awoke in the water tower. Brie was snoring softly, a whistle in her nose with every inhalation. She was curled around the teddy bear, clutching it in her paws like she needed something warm and soft. Curled around her was Penny, probably also asleep, Fin thought. It was hard to tell with the shadow. And sitting on Penny's back was Morri, her head tucked under one wing.

It was cute. It was also sort of terrifying.

Fin rose quietly, bundling the blanket into her backpack. She opened the front door, glanced over her shoulder to make sure the others were still resting. She snapped her fingers. While Brie had to stay here and Penny could slip through any crack, the raven needed to come with Fin.

Morri jerked awake. She looked about blearily, gaze alighting on Fin. Fin held the door open and gestured at it. The raven puffed up her feathers, then stretched her wings and flew outside. She landed on a high branch, croaking quietly to herself. "Yeah, yeah," said Fin, smiling at her. "Sorry, but you can't sleep in today. I need your help."

The walk back to the cottage was brisk and damp. Mist clung to the empty spaces between the trees, and the fallen redwood needles were soft with dew. The sunlight was peeking over the eastern horizon, flooding the cloudy sky with gold. Fin breathed deeply, enjoying the scents of the forest. She liked the woods best in the morning, when everything was still and fresh and quiet. There were only a few people awake— road trippers rousing early to leave Aldermere for their next destination and a handful of those who ran businesses that catered to the morning rush. Fin kept her gaze ahead and hurried down the street, hoping no one would notice the lone girl walking through town so early.

As quietly as she could, Fin toed off her shoes and left them on the cottage porch so Mom wouldn't notice how damp they were. Then she carefully unlocked the cottage's front door and slipped inside. She stepped over two squeaky floorboards before hurrying up the ladder to the loft. Eddie was sprawled on his sleeping bag with his mouth agape and limbs in every direction. Fin slipped out of her coat, put her backpack down, and changed her clothes. "Wake up," she said, nudging Eddie.

He groaned and tried to roll over.

"Morri visited me again last night," said Fin. "I think the SNACC Pack might have found tracks from the bigfoot herd."

That woke him. Eddie came alert with a startled "Wah?"

"Get dressed," said Fin. "I'm going to get us some breakfast."

When Mom came into the kitchen, Fin was eating cereal at the small table while Eddie fumbled to put on his shoes. "Hey," said Mom. She looked startled but not displeased. "You're both up early."

Fin shrugged. "Just woke up. Kind of wanted to get an early start."

"You two have plans?" asked Mom. She reached for the cereal box, pouring her own bowl. "Or did you want to come to work with me? We've got some clean linens that need folding."

"Sorry," said Fin. "Got plans."

When this was over, when Brie was safe with her herd, Fin would spend a day at the inn. She would fold linens and hang out in her mom's office and luxuriate in the reliable routine of the day. But for now, she couldn't.

Today was a day for woods and monsters, for the dark and shadowed places.

Which was how Fin ended up walking toward Brewed Awakening. Eddie had reluctantly agreed to take the first shift with Brie. Mostly because Morri belonged to Fin—or perhaps it was that Fin belonged to Morri. Either way, the raven had never shown an interest in Eddie. Fin promised him that she would return if they found the herd. After all, she would need to retrieve Brie.

At eight in the morning, Brewed Awakening was bustling, outside tables overflowing with people and a line out the door. A familiar green-haired woman sat outside. Ana Bell. Michael sat beside her, and they were huddled over a laptop together.

At this distance, Fin couldn't see what they were looking at. Nor could she eavesdrop on them. It was a relief to see them, because if they were here, then they weren't out in the woods.

Fin waited to walk into the coffee shop. Technically she didn't have to wait—she wasn't planning on buying anything—but she didn't want anyone to think she was cutting in line. When it was her turn, she angled herself through the door and sidestepped the register area. Sure enough, Cedar was behind the counter helping to bag up pastries. When she caught sight of Fin, a smile broke across her face. "Hi."

"Hey," said Fin. Her gaze fell to the floor. Cedar had no shadow. Which meant Penny was still at the water tower.

Fin lowered her voice, leaning around the edge of the pastry display. "Listen," she said. "I've got a lead on where Brie's family might be. Morri found something. You want to come?"

Cedar grimaced. "I can't. I promised to help my parents this morning. Sorry." She looked a little anxious for a moment, as if this refusal might offend Fin.

"I get it," said Fin. "Eddie's going to keep an eye on Brie. You should stop by when you get a chance—I'll let you know what I find."

Cedar nodded. Then she ducked behind the counter and emerged with a small white paper bag. "Old shortbread cookies," she said, pressing them into Fin's hands. "Just in case."

Fin smiled, thanked Cedar, and maneuvered her way out of the busy coffee shop. When she stepped outside, she saw Ana and Michael still at their table. Fin watched them for a few heartbeats, then squared her shoulders and strode away.

She made for the gap between Brewed Awakening and the next house over. There would be a bit of privacy—and Fin didn't want anyone to watch her. When she was sure she was alone, Fin reached into the paper bag and broke off a bit of cookie. She held it up.

She must have looked a little ridiculous: a lone girl, holding a cookie to the sky.

But then there was the *womp-womp* of strong wings slicing through the air, and a dark blur alighted on Fin's hand. Morri awkwardly clung to Fin's wrist, talons finding purchase on her sleeve as she nibbled eagerly at the cookie. Fin let her have the small piece. Then Morri looked around for more.

"Cookie," Fin said. "Footprints. Show me."

Maybe if she kept things simple, "show me" would work better than "fetch."

Morri hopped in place for a moment, and Fin was reminded of dogs begging for treats. When this show of cuteness didn't work, the raven puffed herself into an indignant ball of black feathers, then took to the air. She landed on the roof of the house, glanced back at Fin, and gave a loud, indignant croak.

"I'm coming, I'm coming," said Fin.

Fin quickened her steps, glancing up every so often to see where Morri had landed. The raven flew ahead a few houses, landed—presumably waiting for the clumsy and slow human to keep pace—and then took to the air again.

Talia and Mrs. Brackenbury were drinking tea on the porch swing. Fin offered a quick wave but didn't dare stop for chitchat. Talia's eyes were like a weight, and she only met that watchful gaze for a heartbeat. Morri flew southeast and Fin turned right, toward the fire station. Mrs. Petrichor lived in a cabin behind the station; her familiar minivan had several ravens sitting atop it. They watched with interest as Fin walked by.

Finally the town began to recede.

Several hiking trails began near the southeast edge of town. Many of the old water towers had been converted to vacation rentals, and a self-service information center had brochures about nearby campsites, hiking trails, and museums in the next town over. There was a familiar NO BURNING PERMITS sign too. No matter the season or the level of fire danger, that sign never came down. Burning wasn't allowed within the boundaries of Aldermere, save for a few wood stoves kept by locals and the occasional illicit candle.

Fire could destroy magic. Fire could destroy pretty

much anything. That was something she'd learned living in California; a single lightning strike or party gone awry could ignite a devastating blaze. It was why at the town meeting Mayor Downer had made such a point of saying that the nearby smoke was from a controlled burn; it would keep everyone from calling Mrs. Petrichor in a panic.

Morri landed on one of the hiking trails, eyeing Fin eagerly. "Not yet," said Fin, gesturing with the paper bag. "You'll get this once I see the footprints."

Morri grumbled low in her throat but turned and flapped toward the south trail. Fin took a breath of the crisp morning air, held it in her lungs for a moment, then stepped forward. She had never hiked on her own before. The southern trails were a mix of redwood and Douglas fir. Spring wildflowers brightened the green undergrowth: the white flowers of the salal bushes and the purple wood violets.

Fin walked for perhaps twenty minutes before Morri veered from the path. The raven landed on a young pine, looking back at Fin expectantly.

Fin swallowed and took a breath. Her backpack held a heavy flashlight, a map, and Nick's notes. She was as prepared as she could be.

She stepped from the trail and into the forest. Within a few steps, the forest reached open its arms and enveloped her. She could not see the path, couldn't see any signs of humanity at all.

Fin reached out to a fern and broke the top. She would have to find her way home again, and she wasn't sure she could count on Morri as a guide. The raven meant well, but she could be easily distracted. And forests were tricky things; she'd heard stories of hikers getting lost and not being found for days. And sometimes people just vanished.

The morning was full of the chatter of birds, and the sound made Fin feel braver. Surely nothing truly bad could happen while small fat birds were chirping and whistling at one another.

The undergrowth thinned out a little as she walked into the old-growth forest, where the trees cast long shadows. Fin broke a fern frond every twenty feet or so, trying to keep track of her path.

And then all the birdsong went silent.

Fin slowed, her hand resting lightly on the trunk of a tree as she listened. For a moment, she hoped it was her imagination. But no—the woods had gone quiet as a held breath.

Fin licked her dry lips. She stepped around the tree, moving as soundlessly as she could. Nick had said bigfoots could smell age. She'd heard of dogs smelling fear; maybe if

Fin was unafraid, the bigfoots would be too. She wasn't an adult—she couldn't harm them.

She rounded the tree and found herself gazing at a small field of delicate shield ferns. An old rotting cabin stood beneath a patch of sunlight, its logs crumbling into the ground and moss crawling up its sides. Fin's attention fell on the cabin as she walked closer—so much that she stumbled over the indent in the ground.

She landed on her knees, fingers in the damp and cool earth. And that was how she saw them. They were tucked away, hidden by the meadow of ferns.

Footprints.

If Fin hadn't been looking for them, she might have thought the ground was uneven. But she saw the familiar shape of an almost-human foot. It looked like Brie's—but far larger. Fin traced the edge of one footprint.

"They were here," she whispered. Morri croaked from a branch overhead.

Fin knelt and dug the sheet out of her backpack. Unfolding it, her eyes fell across the words Nick had scribbled across the page in his slanting, slightly uneven handwriting. He had listed a few places that he knew the bigfoots frequented— and the second-to-last line read *South of town, near an old lightning-struck tree and an abandoned cabin.*

This was the spot. The bigfoot herd had been here—and maybe if Fin brought Brie here, they would come back for her. Brie could go home and Aldermere's secrets would be safe.

Elated, Fin let out a small laugh. She dug the rest of the cookie from her coat pocket. "Good girl," said Fin. "Fetch."

She tossed the cookie into the air, and Morri swooped down upon it. The raven picked it up, looked around, then flapped up high to one of the trees. Fin watched her go, wondering why the raven hadn't just eaten the snack right there.

A breeze tugged at Fin's hair, and she pushed the strands out of her eyes as the wind yanked Nick's paper from her loose fingers. Fin grabbed for it, but the sheet fluttered out of reach, tumbling end over end through the ferns. She began to step after it, but then something emerged from the forest.

Fin jerked to a halt, her heart slamming against her ribs. For a moment, her eyes had to strain through the shadows. Then sunlight shone on blond hair and a lightly tanned face, and Ryan Bell stepped into the clearing.

He looked as he had the night Fin had seen him by the old logging road: dressed in a SNACC T-shirt with a jacket and jeans. His expression was watchful and remote.

Fin's mind kicked into overdrive, spitting out thoughts

so fast she could barely keep up. Why was Ryan Bell here? Had he come for these footprints too? Why was he out here and his sister at Brewed Awakening? Had he followed Fin?

But she could ask none of these questions. So she said, "Morning." To her relief, her voice sounded casual.

Ryan held up his hand in greeting. "Good morning," he said with mild surprise. "Did you get separated from your parents?"

Fin shook her head. "I live here," she said. Then she flushed. "Well, not here," she added, with a glance at the cabin. "I live in town. I'm, uh, doing a school project and needed some—" She racked her brain for something believable. "Plants." She ducked down and plucked one of the shield ferns, tucking it into her pocket.

"Ah, I see," said Ryan. His voice was soft and level, and it would have sounded nice if Fin's heart hadn't been pounding so hard. "It's early, isn't it? Don't kids sleep in these days?"

"Too many tourists later in the day," she said.

Ryan smiled. "This doesn't seem like a place many tourists would go."

"You're here," said Fin. Perhaps her counseling was working—or maybe it was the adrenaline that made her bold. The conversation felt like a sword fight in one of Eddie's video games: parry and thrust, every sentence pointed.

Ryan let out a laugh, and it was a good laugh—all rippling amusement and genuine warmth. "That I am," he agreed. "That I am. Well, I'll leave you to your homework, then." He knelt down to reach for the fallen sheet of paper.

Fin drew in a sharp breath and stepped forward to grab it, but Ryan got there first. He picked it up, his eyes roaming over the notes. His smile faded and a line etched itself across his forehead.

"Thanks," said Fin, and snatched the paper from his fingers. She crammed it into her pocket and hurried away.

She expected him to stop her. To demand to see that paper again. She quickened her steps until she was almost jogging; her backpack jounced on her hip, and she clutched at the strap with damp fingers.

She hurried out of the clearing and back into the woods. Only once she was a good forty feet away did she chance a look over her shoulder.

Ryan Bell stood at the edge of the clearing, gently touching one of the sword ferns that Fin had snapped. His fingers brushed across the fronds, and he looked sharply at her. As if in realization.

Fin took a shaky breath and hurried back the way she had come.

SEVENTEEN
Deliveries and Pickups

It took Fin half the time to get back to Aldermere. Her trail of broken ferns led her right to the hiking trail, and from there she jogged most of the way back. When the fire station came into view, her tense stomach collapsed in relief. She relaxed within the boundaries of town, where she was surrounded by familiar people and buildings. Even if Ryan Bell followed her, she was safe here.

Fin glanced at Brewed Awakening. Ana Bell wasn't at her table, and Fin didn't see any of the film crew. River sat at the farthest table, glaring into the contents of his white paper cup. Fin remembered their last encounter and looked away, glad the distance between them was enough that she could pretend not to have seen him.

Hopefully Ryan Bell hadn't spotted the mention of the lightning-struck tree on the paper when he'd glanced over it. And even if he had, Fin told herself, he couldn't guess at its meaning. There wasn't any mention of bigfoot on the sheet—just a list of approved foods and suggestions of hiking locations. It could have looked like something for a school project. Fin hoped that was what Ryan would think.

Plans formed and reformed in her mind. She would need both Eddie and Cedar; moving Brie out into the woods was no easy feat. She would need more snacks, which she could pick up at the Ack. And they were going to need a little luck too.

Fin turned down Main Street toward the Ack. Two tourists stood on the porch, one frowning at a hiking map and the other squatting down to pet the cat. The cat appeared to be enjoying the attention, rolling around on his back and purring loudly. Fin gave them both a polite smile as she veered around them and pushed open the doors. A few more customers meandered through the small aisles and Fin took a step toward the fresh produce, but Mr. Hardin's familiar voice rang out.

"You're early today, Fin," he said. He had been

straightening the brochures by the register. When she froze, he ducked beneath the counter and reappeared with a bundle of boxes.

Oh. It was *Tuesday.* Which meant delivery day. Mr. Hardin thought she was here to pick up her weekly deliveries. And she couldn't think of a way to get out of it. "Right," she said, scrambling for a reply. "Well—um. Spring break and all."

Mr. Hardin handed over four boxes, glancing at the labels. "There's one for the inn, Mrs. Liu's arthritis medication is here, this is for Ms. Catmore, and the last one's for Mrs. Brackenbury."

Fin nodded as she took them. Her mind was already racing, trying to map out the town and its occupants to figure out the best route. Ms. Catmore had a house on the west side of town; Fin could go there first, then right up Main Street and hit Mrs. Liu's, Mrs. Brackenbury's, and lastly the inn.

"Thanks," said Fin. "See you."

Mr. Hardin gave her a friendly wave. "You have a good day, Fin."

Fin hefted the packages into her arms and nudged the door open with her hip. It was almost a relief to fall into the relative ease of delivery day; this was something she knew how to do, where the stakes were relatively low and she knew she could succeed. She trotted down the street, past the Fog & Crown Diner. It was a place meant for tourists rather than locals. The food was expensive and it was designed with faux old-Western décor. Mom had taken Fin there on her last birthday. A few tourists lingered outside, clearly waiting for a table. The smell of warm waffles wafted through the air, and Fin's stomach gurgled.

Ignoring her hunger, Fin made her way to Ms. Catmore's house. Her home was a tiny house. It had wheels and a place where it could be attached to a truck, but judging by the moss growing on the tires, no one had moved it in many years. It was cute—painted blue, with white trim and a little pointed roof. Fin walked up the three steps to the front door and knocked.

There came the sound of heels on linoleum, and then Ms. Catmore opened the door. She had a pencil wedged behind her ear, and her lipstick was carefully in place. "Finley," she said. "You have something for me?"

Fin set down the stack of packages, sliding out the middle box. It had the name of a computer company on it. "This one."

"Oh, thank goodness." Ms. Catmore picked it up with a sigh. "My laptop cord's literally held together with duct tape.

Which I know Petra would hate, if she knew. Fire hazard and all."

Fin nodded, unsure of what to say.

"Hold on a moment." Ms. Catmore ducked into her home. When she returned, she held a copy of the *Aldermere Oracle* and two chocolate chip cookies wrapped in a napkin. Fin took the cookies gratefully and crammed the newspaper into her back pocket. The paper would probably end up as mulch in Aunt Myrtle's garden; no one ever read the news articles, preferring the recipes and occasional anonymous bit of gossip. But somehow the newspapers always appeared, without fail, on people's doorsteps.

Fin's next stop was Mrs. Liu. She had once used the magical tea shop to deal with her chronic arthritis, but ever since the shop had vanished, she'd needed to control it through other means. Fin only knew that because Mr. Hardin ordered her prescriptions, and Fin had been delivering them more often.

It made Fin feel terrible, knowing that someone was suffering because the tea shop was gone.

After she'd delivered the medication, Fin headed for Mrs. Brackenbury's. Mrs. Brackenbury answered the door after Fin had knocked twice. She had a cup of tea in one hand and a rolled-up copy of the *San Francisco Chronicle* tucked under her arm. "Thanks, dear," she said, seeing the box. "Can you put that in the foyer? On that shelf there? Thank you so much."

Mr. Bull sat in the hallway, eyeing Fin hopefully. She squatted down and scratched behind his ears. The dog made a happy little groaning noise and closed his eyes. He was a sweet dog, even if he was too old to go on walks and guard the house from whintossers.

"Would you like to stay for tea?" asked Mrs. Brackenbury.

Fin shook her head. "I've got one more delivery. Maybe next time."

Then she was out of the house and hurrying to the inn. The parking lot was still full, and Fin couldn't help but glance at the SNACC van on the edge of the lot. She ducked around a family and through the inn's doors. Jo was helping a few guests check out, and Fin recognized the bright, cheery tone of voice she used with customers. Fin glanced at the box's label. If there was a particular staff member mentioned, she could bring it to them. But there was nothing. With a calculating glance at the guests, she darted around the line, slipped behind the desk, and said, "Hey, Jo!" She set the box down where it wouldn't be tripped over. "Bye, Jo!" And then she was hurrying away.

Jo gave her a wave before turning back to the customers.

Deliveries finished, Fin let out a sigh of relief. It was a small weight lifted, having one responsibility gone.

When she returned to the water tower, Fin found Eddie and Brie sitting beneath it.

"She didn't like being indoors so much," said Eddie. He was playing with Brie, waving a fern frond so she would try and catch it. The bigfoot circled him, her dark eyes intent on the frond and her whiskers twitching. "So I brought her down again."

"I get it," said Fin. She leaned against one of the tower's legs, glad for a chance to stop moving. "She's used to being outside all the time." She glanced around. "Did you see Penny?"

"Was she here?" Eddie waggled the fern frond along the forest floor. Brie made a grab for it and missed.

"All last night," said Fin. "Maybe she left after I did. Cedar's at Brewed Awakening, helping her parents. But we'll need to grab her before we return Brie to the herd."

Eddie's eyes lit up. "You found them?"

Fin told him everything. When she was finished, he was so distracted that Brie easily snatched the fern from his fingers. She waved it herself, looking pleased.

"Okay," said Eddie quietly, as if he spoke to himself. "So

we take her to the southeast trail." He looked at Brie. "Later today?"

"Maybe around five?" said Fin. "The coffee shop closes then."

Eddie nodded in agreement. "You want to go tell Cedar?"

Fin made a face. Her legs ached and all she wanted to do was sit down. "Can you do it? I need a break from running everywhere. We also need more snacks," she added.

Eddie huffed out an amused breath. "That I can do." He heaved himself upright. "I'll tell Cedar the plan, then stop for some bigfoot snacks. You want anything? A sandwich?"

"Sure." Fin sat on the ground near Brie. The bigfoot waved the fern frond at her, and Fin smiled. "Meet back here?"

"See you soon," said Eddie. He turned to go, then went still.

"What is it?" asked Fin uneasily.

Eddie squinted at the forest. "Just . . . thought I saw something moving." He took a step forward, then shook his head. "Never mind. It's not an animal—must be Penny."

Fin had never questioned how Eddie knew things about animals: where to find them, what they were feeling, what they wanted. It had always been an Eddie thing. But it was comforting to know that his intuition had some limits. And it looked like magical shadows were that limit.

Eddie turned toward town. "I'll be back in an hour, probably." He ruffled Brie's ears and ambled away from the water tower.

Brie watched him go, the fern slipping from her paws. She picked up her teddy bear and began trying to smooth the bear's whiskers.

Fin looked toward the forest. "Penny? That you?" She waited for the shadow horse to ghost through the woods, but she never appeared. Maybe she was returning to Cedar or patrolling the nearby forest.

Fin played with Brie for the better part of an hour. When she tired of trying to catch the fern, Brie curled up beside Fin's leg, using her shin as a pillow. The bigfoot blinked sleepily up at her.

She was going to miss Brie when this was all over. The bigfoot was cute and sweet. Maybe Fin would talk to Mom about getting a cat. The one at the Ack liked Fin; maybe a cat would enjoy living in the cottage. There was a bookshelf Fin could empty out, put a cat bed in place of old paperback mysteries. And they could fit a litter box beside their own toilet in the bathroom.

Fin was considering how best to ask Mom when Brie suddenly lifted her head. She sniffed the air.

"Is Eddie coming back with food?" asked Fin. "You smelling grilled cheese?"

Brie sniffed a second time, her small ears pricked forward. She rose to her feet, paws tucked against her stomach as she peered at the forest.

"Eddie?" said Fin. But there was no reply. Frowning, she pushed herself upright. Her legs were a little stiff after sitting so long. Brie made a noise that Fin had never heard before: a soft whining. Like a question. Fin put her hand on Brie's head, hoping to soothe her.

There was a clicking sound—the unmistakable whisper of a camera shutter. Fin's head jerked up and she looked around wildly. It took her eyes a second to fall upon the figure twenty feet away. He was lean and tall, one camera dangling from the holster beneath one shoulder. Another camera was in his hand. And it was aimed directly at Fin and Brie. His shirt had a bright, clearly printed logo.

SNACC.

Michael was in the bushes. Michael was taking pictures of Brie. Fin's lungs froze and her blood turned to ice.

"No." The word came out small and breathy. Fin held out one hand as if to beseech Michael to put down the camera. She took a step toward him, so that she stood between the camera and Brie.

But that was a mistake.

Someone else burst from the ferns to her left. Footsteps pounded against the ground, and Brie let out a shriek. It was a yelp of pure fear, sharp against Fin's eardrums. Someone knocked into Fin and drove her to the ground; she landed heavily on her hands and knees.

She looked up in time to see Ryan Bell throw a net over Brie. When the bigfoot tried to run, the plastic caught in her feet and tripped her. She shrieked again, thrashing wildly.

"Hand me the bag, kid," said Ryan sharply.

And then a third figure emerged from the bushes.

River.

His glasses had slipped down his nose. He was holding a burlap sack as he hurried beneath the water tower. He shot one worried glance at the bigfoot writhing under the net, but he didn't look at Fin.

Ryan didn't hesitate as he hefted the net and bigfoot into the bag. At once the bag began to squirm. River took several steps back, as if repulsed.

"Stop," cried Fin. She rose to her feet. "You're hurting her!"

Ana Bell stepped out of the shadow of a redwood tree, her dyed green hair gleaming in the sunlight. Her face was lit with a terrible wonder, her eyes never leaving the bag.

"I can't believe it," she said quietly. "The kid was right."

"I knew it," said Ryan. "I told you this place was different. I knew it."

"You did," said Ana. "I'll give you that."

River retreated another few steps. "So I get the reward money?" he asked. His voice was subdued, and he still wouldn't look at Fin.

"Yes, of course," said Ana. "We honor our promises."

A fury like Fin had never known roared through her. She whirled on River and in that moment, she wasn't sure what her face looked like. All she knew was that she wanted to be terrifying. She must have succeeded because River staggered away from her, his own face bloodless. His foot hit a tree root and he fell backward, his glasses landing amid the redwood needles.

"You," snarled Fin.

That was all it took. River pushed himself upright, turned, and sprinted away from the water tower. He was gone in a matter of moments.

Ana squatted beside the wriggling sack. "Did you get pictures, Michael?"

"Got 'em," said Michael. He jogged closer, angling his camera so that Ana could see its screen. "The girl and the creature. This is going to make those Cottingley fairies look like a blip on the radar."

Ana knelt beside the bag. She held her hand over the sack, close but not quite touching. Then she straightened. "Let's get this thing back to the van. We're checking out tonight. Email Talbot as soon as we get back to the hotel. I'm not sure if UCLA will let us use their labs again after that squirroose incident, but maybe if we promise them a mention in our Nobel speech . . ."

"No," cried Fin. She lunged forward, but someone caught her by the back of the shirt. It was Ryan, holding her in place. "You can't take her away. Her family—"

"You're lucky we showed up when we did," said Ryan. "A wild animal like that could have hurt you."

"She's not dangerous," said Fin. She threw herself to one side and heard the sound of ripping fabric. Ryan released her.

Fin hit the ground hard. She pushed herself to her elbows, heart hammering. She had gone from icy cold to burning hot in a matter of seconds as anger swept through her. How dare they—how dare these people bag up Brie like she was a prize to be found? They were going to take her away? Fin wouldn't let them.

Fin tried to dart around Ryan, to make a grab for the bag.

If she could free Brie, then the bigfoot might be able to make a run for it. The film crew didn't know these woods, couldn't follow quickly enough to keep up with a wild animal. All Fin had to do was—

But the bag was already being lifted into the air by Ana Bell. She hefted it over her shoulder.

Fin started to run after Ana, but Ryan shoved her. Fin hit the ground a second time, the jolt running up her elbows. Tears sprang to her eyes—tears of frustration and anger. She was too small, too powerless. All she could do was listen to the sound of Brie screaming with fear as she was carried away.

EIGHTEEN
Brie-vengers, Assemble!

For a few moments, Fin could not move. She knelt on the redwood needles, beneath the shadow of a water tower.

She had lost Brie.

She had lost Brie.

The SNACC Pack would take Brie down to Los Angeles and study her, figure out that she wasn't anything humanity had ever encountered before. Aldermere would be overrun with scientists, with gawkers, with hunters. The bigfoot herd would be driven back into the wilderness; the town would be picked apart and put under a microscope. The magic would be drained, and it would be the end of Aldermere—of home, of everything that Fin had tried to protect. She yearned to go ten minutes back in time, to do something that could have averted all of this. But she couldn't—and she was just a kid. A kid couldn't stop three adults, not even three young adults, from kidnapping Brie.

Despair swept in. Fin let out a ragged breath and squeezed her eyes shut.

Come on. The words came from deep within her. That voice was quiet and resolute, and Fin recognized it. She had heard it before: a voice that was both hers and not hers. *Teafin.* She had been made of bad memories, of anger and sadness and defiance—all the pieces of herself that Fin had once tried to forget. But she was also the voice of reckless bravery, of a girl who'd been a little wicked and fearless.

Right now, Brie needed that girl.

Ana had mentioned emailing someone. And River—

River.

The moment Fin thought the name, her anger flared even hotter. River had led them to Brie. He must have followed Fin to the water tower. It hadn't been Penny that Eddie had glimpsed in the woods—it had been River. And then he'd led the SNACC Pack here.

Fin picked up River's fallen glasses. They were black rimmed, smudged a little at one corner. Rising to her feet, she turned toward town and began to run.

/ / /

"I'm gonna take all of River's homework and dump it in a mud puddle," said Eddie, his face alight with fury.

They jogged down Main Street. Fin had found Eddie back at the cottage, where he'd been preparing several sandwiches. Fin had explained the situation in gasps, but he'd understood enough to be angrier than she'd ever seen him.

"Revenge later," said Fin. "Brie now. You grab Cedar and I'll go to River's house. He might know what SNACC's planning."

"I am going," replied Eddie, "to find something that smells really, really bad and put it in his locker every day for the rest of the year."

"I'm fine with that," said Fin.

Eddie continued to mutter threats until they parted ways. Eddie headed toward Brewed Awakening, while Fin veered toward River's house. The porch still held several unpacked boxes. Fin hesitated, then knocked on the front door. There was no answer, and after a minute she peered through a window and saw an empty living room—a few paintings leaned against the walls and there was a half-assembled coffee table, but no people. She darted around to the back of the house.

The old burned shed had been torn down. There was a

spot of dead grass where it had once stood. Someone had strung a clothesline from an apple tree to the house, and several shirts were drying in an afternoon breeze. A bench had been placed near the back of the house—and River sat on it. When he caught sight of Fin, he shrank back.

Fin's anger, which she'd managed to tamp down, roiled to the surface. She strode across the backyard, hands clenched into fists.

"Why?" she snarled. "Why did you do it?"

River didn't stand up. "Do what?" He looked younger without his glasses. Less certain of himself.

"You went to the film crew," she said. "You told them about Brie!"

River swallowed audibly and his gaze skittered to one side. As if he couldn't bear to meet her eyes. Ashamed, she realized. He was ashamed.

"They were offering a cash reward," he said tonelessly. "For proof of cryptid sightings. And—and someone had to know. That thing . . . you can't keep that for a pet. Whatever it is, it's wrong, it's—"

"She," said Fin harshly. "Brie isn't an it, she's a she. And she's a *baby*. Don't you get that? She's a baby, and now the film crew took her. They're going to drag her off to some lab."

River's gaze jerked to meet hers. "What? They said—they said they wanted pictures. Study it for a while. They didn't say they were going to take it."

"Well, Ana Bell lied." Fin crossed her arms over her chest. "She's taking the bigfoot to Los Angeles to study. Brie was crying the whole way—and now she'll never see her family again. That's what we were doing, you know. Trying to get a baby back to her family without someone like you screwing it up!"

River flinched. "Maybe people should know. This place . . . it's wrong. It's weird and dangerous and—"

"It's Aldermere!" said Fin. "And just because you don't understand this town doesn't mean there's something wrong with it. You can't barge in here and think you know better than everyone else! Things can be dangerous, yes. But it's also beautiful and wonderful, and maybe you'd figure that out if you gave it a chance! Or talked to anyone without being a jerk."

"I never asked to come here!" cried River. His frustration seemed to boil over. "I didn't have a choice."

"Neither did I," said Fin. "But you know what? Coming here was the best thing that ever happened to me."

That silenced him. River looked up at her, his face oddly exposed. With a huff, Fin held out his glasses. He blinked, surprised. Then he took them and slid them on.

"I'm sorry," he finally said. "If that means anything."

"Are you?" came Eddie's voice. He and Cedar rounded the corner of the house, walking into the backyard. "You know those sad commercials you see about polar bear pups separated from their parents and stuff? Well, congrats. That's going to be the bigfoot baby, thanks to you."

"I didn't mean to—" River cut himself off. "I thought it was a weird animal and if the film crew was paying people for pictures of weird stuff, then—"

"She's a living creature," said Cedar hotly, taking a step closer. River cringed. "She's got a family, a home. And now she's never going to see them again. That's on you, Scott."

Fin expected River to protest, to try and make excuses. A hot flush spilled across his face, but all he did was nod. "I know." He closed his eyes. "If you're going to hurt me again, just do it."

Cedar took a step back in surprise. "Why would I . . . oh, come on." She reached down and tapped River lightly on his shoulder. "Look at me."

He didn't look at her. Instead, his thumb roamed across a thin scab along his knuckles—where Penny's mane had cut him, Fin realized.

"I don't want to hurt you," said Cedar. "I don't want

to hurt anyone. And I'm sorry that happened. It was an accident. My shadow—her name is Penny. When you called me a freak, I got angry and she reacted. I apologize."

River finally looked up. "What was she?" he said helplessly.

There was so much to explain and so little time. Fin said the only thing she could think of. "Magic," she said.

Several emotions darted across River's face: denial, confusion, and finally an almost irritated acceptance. "I hate that that's the only answer to make sense." He took a deep breath. "Why are you here?"

"Because we need to know where SNACC might've taken Brie," said Eddie. "She's going to be yelling the whole time."

"Not inside the inn," said Fin. "Jo wouldn't stand for it."

River sat a little straighter. "Their van," he said. "I've seen the inside. It's mostly full of equipment and stuff, but it's the only place they trust. It's soundproofed too. For recording. They could put a screaming animal in there and no one would ever know."

"We have to move fast," said Fin. "Before they leave—or before the others hear Brie."

Cedar nodded. "Do you think the other bigfoots will come for her?"

"Maybe," said Eddie, "if she was loud enough before they put her in the van. But what if they leave before the bigfoot army can arrive?"

River went even paler. "Bigfoot army?"

"Yes, and they're coming for you," said Eddie, without missing a beat. "So worst case scenario is a bunch of angry bigfoots show up, looking for their lost kid, and she isn't here anymore."

"We won't let that happen," said Fin determinedly. "Cedar, can you check the van? See if they have Brie in there?"

Cedar nodded.

"Good," said Fin. "Eddie, you're going with her. Watch her back. I'm going to make sure that they don't upload their pictures."

"How?" asked Eddie.

Fin smiled, and she knew it wasn't a very nice smile. "The only place in town they can get online is the inn. Or at least . . . until I stop them."

River pushed himself off the bench. "What can I do?"

That stopped all of them in their tracks.

"What?" said Eddie incredulously. "You want to help? Why should we trust you?"

River gave a helpless little shrug. "I can't make things worse now, can I?"

"I'm sure you could find a way," said Eddie.

River didn't defend himself; he merely stood there, accepting all of their anger. And it was that and that alone that made Fin want to trust him. Bad people found excuses. But River wasn't even trying to defend himself.

"SNACC trusts him," said Fin. "We could use that."

Eddie looked at her sharply. "You've got to be kidding!"

"This isn't about you," she snapped. "I get it. You don't like him. I'm not his biggest fan either, but we don't have a choice! Not if we want to save Brie!"

River raised his hand a little. Like a kid waiting to be called on.

"What?" said Fin irritably.

River put his hand down. "I—I wanted to know why you named the bigfoot after cheese?"

For a moment, they were all silent. And then Cedar let out a half laugh, half snort. And then Fin was smiling and even Eddie started laughing. It broke the tension, and Fin's shoulders relaxed and her breath came a little easier.

"We'll explain on the way," said Fin. She looked at the others. "Unless you think we shouldn't bring him."

Cedar gave a little shrug. "I think we're going to need all the help we can get."

"And you?" said Fin to Eddie. He was frowning like

he'd been asked to eat a bowl of dirt for dinner.

"Fine," he said. "But I'm still going to sabotage his locker at some point."

"I can live with that," said River.

They split up.

Eddie and Cedar headed toward the inn's parking lot. River went with Fin, because teaming up Eddie with his archrival didn't seem like a good idea. She and River veered around the inn, going near the garbage bins and the back entrance.

"Are we allowed to be here?" asked River, eyeing the EMPLOYEES ONLY—INN ENTRANCE sign.

"Yes," said Fin, pulling it open and gesturing him through. "My mom's the assistant manager. And besides, the label's just so people don't pop out somewhere else."

River blinked at her. "They *what*?"

"Magic," said Fin. "I'll explain the rules later."

"Rules," said River, sounding relieved. "There are rules?"

Fin pressed a finger to her lips. She tried to walk as quickly as she could without drawing attention. One of the cleaners ambled by with a cart full of clean linens, and Fin gave her a small wave. As soon as they were alone again, Fin darted into the next hallway.

To her relief, the storage closet wasn't locked. She pulled it open and stepped inside. River hesitated, then followed and pulled the door shut behind them. A buzzing light flickered on overhead.

The wireless router was on one of the plastic shelves in the farthest corner. The router's green lights blinked merrily. Fin gazed at it for a heartbeat. "You know how to do this?" asked River. "Sabotage the internet?"

"Sure," said Fin, and reached down to unplug it. "Not everything has to be complicated."

"I guess," said River with a small laugh. "But how long until someone fixes it?"

"First people will have to figure out it's down," said Fin. "And then someone'll complain to Jo, the lady at the front desk. She'll finish whatever she's doing at her desk. Trust me, she's not a big fan of pushy customers. We've got time."

River nodded, seemingly impressed by Fin's grasp of the situation. Fin led them back through the side entrance; the last thing she wanted was to run into any of the SNACC Pack. She walked quietly around the garbage bins, peering into the parking lot. There was a family unloading a few suitcases from a truck, a couple walking arm in arm toward town, and the SNACC van across the lot. No one was near it.

"Come on," Fin whispered. "Follow me." She darted to the first car, keeping it between her and the inn in case anyone walked outside. They crossed the lot in bursts of speed, pausing to make sure no one was watching. Finally they approached the van. Cedar was crouched in the bushes nearby.

"Hey," said Fin quietly.

Cedar looked up. She flashed Fin a small smile. "Hey."

"Where's Eddie?" asked Fin, glancing around. There was no sign of her cousin.

"Near the lobby doors," answered Cedar. "If the SNACC Pack starts to come out, he'll walk out and cough loudly."

"What'd you find?" asked Fin.

"I think she's in there," said Cedar, throwing a look at the van. "But I'm not entirely sure."

"Would they leave her?" asked River. "I mean, you're not supposed to leave a dog in a car, never mind a . . . *bigfoot.*" It sounded as though saying the word cost him something. "Wouldn't they leave at least one of them to keep an eye on her?"

"Michael," said Cedar. "He's in the passenger seat up front. We saw him get in. It sounded like Ana and Ryan went inside to get their stuff and check out."

Fin bit her lip. Michael would complicate things.

"We need to lure him out," said River. "Distract him."

"I can do that," said Cedar airily. "I'm forgettable."

"But what if they believe in magic now?" said Fin. "They've seen Brie."

"They could just think she's a wild animal," replied Cedar. She took a deep breath. "Trust me, I've got this."

"Okay," Fin said. Because she did trust Cedar.

Cedar rose and stepped out from behind the bushes. She walked around the van, right up to the passenger side. Fin couldn't see through the windows—they were all tinted black. Cedar rapped several times on the door. There was no reply. She rapped again.

The door opened a crack, and Fin heard the voice from inside. "Yes?"

"Hey," said Cedar. Her voice was pitched high, excited. "I heard you're paying for cryptids!"

There was a pause. "Yes, we are," said Michael, and there was a note of apology in his voice. "But we're busy at the moment and—"

"Please," said Cedar. "It will only take a moment. My family could use the money and . . ." She let her voice trail off.

There was a sigh, and then the van door opened fully. Michael stepped out. He looked strange without his holster of cameras. Shutting the van door, he took two steps toward Cedar. "Let's see your pictures."

Cedar looked up at him. Her eyes glittered. "I don't have a picture."

"But you said—" Michael began to say.

"I have a cryptid," said Cedar. "I want you to see it."

Michael clearly thought this was either a prank or some kid trying to con a reward out of him. His brows swept upward, and he shoved his hands in his pockets. "Yeah? Where is it?"

"Right here," said Cedar. She took a deeper breath, closing her eyes. She knelt and pressed both hands to the pavement. To her shadow. She rose, and the darkness followed.

Michael stumbled back, his eyes wide as Cedar's shadow changed. And to be fair, with that uncanny slant to her shoulders and her lack of eyes, Penny did look rather terrifying. The enormous, unsettling shadow stood over Cedar, her mane drifting in a nonexistent breeze.

"What," said Michael faintly, "the—"

Fin wondered what it was like to find out about magic the way River and Michael had—not the gentle introduction that Fin had experienced, with whintossers and magical tea, but with the sudden realization that monsters were real.

Penny reared up. Her hooves were sharp as daggers, her head tossing menacingly. She made no sound, none at all, which was even more nightmarish. And when she landed, one of her hooves cracked the pavement.

Cedar grinned.

Michael choked on his words. He recoiled so fast he nearly fell, his expression aghast. With a breathless little cry, he turned and fled, not bothering to look back. He sprinted away from the van and the inn, a blur that vanished in the direction of town.

Cedar watched him go with a satisfied look. "Well, that should give us a little time." She glanced at Penny. "Mind hiding in the woods, in case any of the inn's other guests walk out?"

Penny tossed her head and jauntily trotted into the woods, as if she was pleased with herself.

River was frozen beside Fin, his eyes fixed on the horse. "That thing's her shadow?"

"Yes," said Fin. "And why you shouldn't cross bridges without knowing the toll first."

"Why . . ." River began to say, but Fin ignored him. She hurried to the back of the van and rose to her tiptoes, trying to see inside. All she could see was her own worried reflection in the glass. Her sweat-slick fingers slid along the van's back door as she tried the handle. Of course it didn't open; the SNACC Pack would have made sure it was locked. The panic Fin had been holding at bay threatened to rise up in her chest, throbbing like a fresh bruise.

"Brie's in there," said Fin. "We have to get her out."

"We can't break a window," said Cedar. "It'll probably start an alarm."

River gazed at the van, then walked right up to the passenger door and pulled on the handle. It opened easily. He leaned in. A moment later, the van's back doors popped open.

Fin and Cedar stared at him.

"What?" said River. "He left it unlocked. And our moving van had the same feature."

"You are officially forgiven," said Fin. Relief made her legs feel shaky. Without hesitating, Fin grabbed the edge of the van and hauled herself inside.

The van had been turned into a recording studio: there was a built-in desk, a laptop, several shelves of recording equipment and lights and cords. A familiar holster with twin cameras hanging from the sides was draped over one of the seats.

On the floor was the sack. It had been tied shut several times, and Fin's fingers slipped on the plastic rope. A soft whining sound came from inside the bag, and it twitched.

"Hey," said Fin. "Hey, it's me. You're okay. I promise we're getting you out."

She glanced around, and her gaze fell on a pair of scissors hanging from a hook on the wall. She seized them, kneeling beside the bag. It wasn't easy to cut open; the burlap was thick and Fin feared accidentally hurting Brie. But after a few tries, she managed to cut a wide enough swath so she could dig her hands in and rip it wide open. The plastic net was easier to cut.

And then Brie was spilling out, all big feet and wide dark eyes. She looked around wildly, her ears pressed tightly to her head.

"It's me," said Fin, holding out her fingers. Brie looked at her and meeped.

Fin's heart cracked a little at the sound. "Come on," she said. "We have to go. I promise we're going to get you back to your family—"

"Oh no," came Cedar's voice. Fin went still. "They're coming." Cedar stuck her head in and said, "Hold on a second," and carefully almost shut the van doors, leaving them open a scant inch.

Breathing hard, Fin crouched and peered through that inch.

Two familiar figures were striding out of the inn. Ryan and Ana Bell.

They were coming this way. Fin swallowed hard, unsure of what to do. They were only forty feet from the van, winding their way through the other cars. Should she and Brie make a run for it? Could Cedar use Penny? Or maybe Fin would have to yell for help, to get her mom out here for backup.

But before Fin could do anything, River sprinted across the lot. He planted himself in front of the SNACC Pack, speaking so loudly that she heard every word.

"Hey," he said. "You're supposed to pay me."

The film crew halted in surprise.

"Oh," said Ana, impatient. "Mr. Rivers, right? Of course we're going to pay you. We took down your mailing address and a check will be in the mail—"

"Do you think I'm stupid?" demanded River. "You think you can placate me because I'm a kid, say you're going to pay me, then send a T-shirt in the mail as compensation? You're going to pay me now, understand? I want five hundred dollars. Or else I'll go on your website and comment on every video, saying you needed an eleven-year-old to find your monster for you."

That got their attention.

Which was precisely the point, Fin realized. River was

delaying them, making a fuss so that Brie could escape.

"Come on," whispered Fin, reaching for Brie. The bigfoot looked as though she didn't want to be picked up, but she was too frightened to protest. Fin hefted the bigfoot into her arms as Cedar carefully edged the van door open. Fin jumped down, keeping a tight hold on Brie. It was a bit like holding a very soft, long dog. Albeit one with feet that were gently thudding against Fin's thighs like swim fins.

Cedar darted around to the front of the van. "What are you doing?" hissed Fin.

Cedar ducked inside, then emerged with the holster of twin cameras. She hastily slung it over her own shoulders and gave Fin a significant look.

The pictures. The evidence. "Good thinking," Fin mouthed.

Keeping low to the ground, they sprinted to the next car over, putting it between them and the SNACC Pack. River was still loudly demanding money while Ana spoke in low, soothing tones. Fin looked around. They needed to get into the forest, where SNACC wouldn't see them.

Fin glanced deliberately at the trees, and Cedar nodded in understanding.

With Brie over one shoulder, Fin scuttled toward the woods. As soon as the trees closed around her, she straightened and began to run. Cedar kept pace behind her. They moved as quickly and as quietly as possible, struggling through the undergrowth until they met the trail.

And then somewhere in the parking lot behind them, a cry rang out.

NINETEEN
In for a Penny

Fin did not look back. She kept all her attention on the trail, on where to put her feet. There was no time for mistakes, no margin for error. She had to get Brie to safety. The bigfoot was a heavy weight against her shoulder, but Fin barely felt the burden; adrenaline flared through her in painfully hot bursts, pushing back any discomfort.

Shouts came from behind, yells mingled with anger and panic. Ana Bell had lost the most valuable cryptozoological find in the history of . . . well, *ever*. And she would be desperate to get it back.

Fin lengthened her stride. Sprinting wasn't possible in a forest, not with the slick redwood needle trails, the fallen branches, and the fern fronds. To run would have been to invite disaster. So Fin moved as fast as she dared, hiking quickly up the familiar hill. The trail wound back and forth, ascending deeper into the old-growth forest.

Brie whined softly in Fin's ear, and she stroked the bigfoot's back, hoping that the creature wouldn't try to bolt. "It's okay," Fin panted, breathless. "It's okay." She chanced a look back.

Cedar was behind Fin, her face set in determined lines. Her shadow was gone—Penny was somewhere in the woods.

And as she glanced back at Cedar, Fin caught sight of a figure bolting up the trail. He burst through the foliage like a deer, all long legs and speed. Sunlight caught on blond hair, and Fin's heart lurched.

Ryan Bell.

He was catching up—fast. He had the advantage of longer legs and no burden to carry. He looked up and saw them, his eyes hard and chest heaving.

Fin turned her head away and pumped her legs even faster. Her muscles burned as she hastened up the steep hill; once, her foot slipped and she had to catch herself with her free hand. Brie whimpered, and Fin tucked her even closer, straightening and climbing on.

They reached the top of the hill; Fin's lungs felt sandpaper raw, and Cedar was gasping for breath. But they couldn't stop. Fin could hear the pounding footsteps behind them.

"We aren't going to be able to outrun him," Fin said raggedly. "Not like this."

"I'm open to suggestions," Cedar panted.

Fin racked her brain. They didn't have bicycles—and it would've been too dangerous to ride them anyway. They could veer from the path, but Fin wasn't sure they wouldn't end up lost. They needed a way to move faster than Ryan and his sister. They needed—

"Penny," breathed Fin.

Cedar looked at her sharply. "What?"

"Penny," repeated Fin. "You said you tried to ride her once. Do you think . . . ?"

Fin watched as understanding dawned behind Cedar's eyes, swiftly followed by fear. "I—I don't know if she would—"

"We have to try," said Fin. She heard the drumbeat of footsteps, the crashing through branches. Ryan was gaining fast.

Cedar bit her lip, expression torn. Then she squeezed her eyes and fists shut, as if she were concentrating very hard.

For a heartbeat, nothing happened. And then a shadow

flickered out of the corner of Fin's eye. Penny cantered out of the trees, tail held high. She regarded Fin and Cedar with her eyeless stare. "Penny," said Cedar, and her voice was wavering. "We need you." She reached out as if to take hold of Penny's mane.

Penny danced away, suddenly skittish.

Cedar's hand fell to her side. "You should take Brie and run. I'll try and delay Ryan and Ana. Maybe Penny will scare them too."

"They could hurt you," said Fin.

Cedar shook her head.

Fin glanced farther down the trail. Part of her yearned to keep going, to let Cedar deal with the SNACC Pack. But she couldn't. She wouldn't abandon Cedar. She took hold of Cedar's hand with her own, squeezing tight.

"No," Fin said. "I'm not leaving you alone."

Something in the words sent a shock through Cedar's expression. She looked down at Fin's hand. A ripple ran across Penny's form, like water disturbed by a falling stone. Cedar took one unsteady breath and then another. Her gaze darted toward Fin, then landed on Penny.

"I'm not alone," Cedar whispered. "I'm not. I'm *not*."

She stepped closer to the horse, slipping from Fin's grasp, and this time there was no hesitation. Cedar touched the horse's nose. "Hey, Penny," she said. Her voice was quiet but sure. "I need a ride."

The shadow monster nuzzled Cedar's fingers, then lowered its front legs, as if in a bow.

Unafraid, Fin realized. Because there was no fear in Cedar for the shadow to echo.

Cedar grasped the shadowy tendrils of mane and hauled herself across its back. "Get on," she said, holding out a hand.

Fin took Cedar's hand, keeping her other arm firmly wrapped around Brie as she slid onto Penny's back.

Fin had been on a pony once before. At a petting zoo when she was seven and lived in Modesto. That animal had been sleepy eyed, flicking its tail at flies and plodding along on a lead while Fin grasped at the saddle horn for dear life. She'd never been a fan of big animals, but at least that pony had been reassuringly old and lazy.

When Penny rose to her full height, Fin's stomach swooped uneasily. With her free arm, Fin held tight to Cedar's shirt. Cedar buried her hands in the horse's inky mane, leaned down, and whispered, "Run."

And then they were *flying*.

Well, some distant, rational part of Fin noted, they weren't really flying. But it *felt* like it. The shadow bolted down the trail. They galloped through the woods, and ferns whipped at Fin's legs and the wind snagged in her hair. Fin desperately wished she had something sturdier to cling to, and Brie seemed to share that opinion. Her tiny claws hooked themselves into Fin's shirt, and the bigfoot buried her face in Fin's neck.

Behind them came a startled shout. Fin shot a look over her shoulder and saw Ryan Bell standing at the crest of the hill, gazing down at them as the shadow tore through the undergrowth. His face was bloodless, but his eyes burned with a terrible light. He yelled something that Fin couldn't catch, because within seconds Ryan had vanished behind the trees. A wild joy made Fin laugh, but even that sound was captured by the wind.

It wasn't only that Penny was fast, although she was. It was that the shadow moved through the trees without fear of stumbling. She navigated these woods the same way Fin could navigate the cottage. Penny left the hiking trail behind, flitting over fallen logs and through narrow spaces where no true horse could have fit.

The forest belonged to the monsters and the monsters belonged to the forest.

Buoyed by the exhilaration of escape, Fin closed her eyes for a moment. They had done it. They had saved Brie. They even had the cameras.

But it wasn't enough. Fin knew it wasn't enough. The SNACC Pack might have uploaded those photos already. And if they didn't have evidence, Ana Bell and her brother would never rest now that they'd found something real.

Fin had seen that terrible, hungry look before—standing outside a tea shop, facing another young man driven by desperation and greed. Ryan wouldn't give up. He would come back and bring more people with him. They would delve into Aldermere with fresh enthusiasm.

Fin had to face one painful truth: Brie had been saved, but Aldermere was still at risk.

Penny slowed to a bumpy trot, then to a steadier walk. Fin sat up and released her painful grip on Cedar's shirt. Brie made a soft, questioning noise and pulled back from Fin, looking around the forest. Cedar patted the horse's neck.

"Now what?" said Cedar. "Should we try and get Brie back where her family is?"

Fin chewed on her lip. It was a tempting thought. "No," she finally said. "Even if Ryan can't follow us, he knows where that field is. He might put everything together." She looked around the forest to figure out where they had ended up. There was the faint sound of trickling water—Bower's Creek, probably. They weren't far north enough for the river.

The river.

An idea occurred to Fin.

It was a terrible idea, the kind that made her a person who belonged with the forest monsters.

"They're never going to stop," said Fin. "Not until they find something. So—so we have to make sure they can't."

Cedar turned to look at her, an unspoken question in her eyes.

"Take Penny back on the trail," said Fin. "Slower, so if Ryan catches up, he can see us. But don't let him catch us."

"Where are we going?" asked Cedar.

Very deliberately, Fin reached down. There was a large sword fern, pristine and reaching for the sunlight. Fin took hold of the biggest frond and broke it. "The toll bridge."

She expected Cedar to argue, but the other girl nodded. She ran her fingers across Penny's neck and whispered a command. The horse tossed her head and began walking toward the trail, parallel to the creek. Every few steps, Fin broke another fern frond.

A trail—but this time, it wasn't for her.

They trotted west along the bank of the creek until the forest fell away and the old logging road and toll bridge stood before them. The afternoon light was beginning to wane as the sun fell beyond the trees. Long shadows stretched across the gravel, and a few ravens watched from a nearby tree.

None of them, Fin realized, had landed on the bridge.

"We need to get across the river," said Fin. "Not using the bridge, obviously."

"This way," said Cedar, nudging at their shadowed mount. Penny shook her mane, veering to the right. Fin clung on with her legs, her fingers digging into Cedar's side as the shadow trotted down the bank of the Eel River. It wasn't easy to keep her balance when the horse tilted forward, but Fin managed to hold on.

The water came up to the horse's belly, brushing Fin's booted feet. The clear, cool river eddied around the shadow, and a few fish swirled by, as if unsure what to make of the intruder.

Penny heaved herself from the water and up the bank on the other side. Once they were on sturdy ground, Fin said, "Stop."

Cedar halted the horse with a touch of her fingers. Penny danced uneasily in place, her gaze turning toward the bridge. Fin wondered if perhaps the shadow knew how close they were to the magic that had made her.

"Take Brie," said Fin, and awkwardly managed to pass the bigfoot over to Cedar. "Ride into the woods and hide there. I have to do this."

Cedar nodded. "Are you sure?"

"Yes." There was no time for hesitation; Fin didn't know how far back Ryan had fallen. He could be here in a matter of minutes. "Can I have the cameras?"

Confusion clouded Cedar's expression, but she slid the holster off and held it out. "Don't cross," she warned.

"I won't," Fin replied. She took the cameras, swung her leg over the side of the horse, and dropped to the ground. It wasn't a graceful landing; she nearly fell onto her knees. The ground was wonderfully steady beneath her, unlike the rocking of the horse.

Cedar squeezed her legs around Penny's sides, and the shadow trotted toward the tree line. Fin jogged toward the toll bridge. It spread out before her, all old redwood. She walked right up to the edge of the bridge, but she didn't step onto it.

Fin stood there, her breathing a little uneven. She had to make this look real enough that none of the SNACC Pack would question it. So while she had no idea how to use them, Fin held one of the cameras as if she was looking at the screen.

And then she waited.

It felt like a few hours passed, but it was probably more like five minutes. Every second, Fin thought of how this plan could go awry. If Ryan didn't find her broken-fern trail or if maybe they decided to call in backup or if they took their anger out on River or Eddie—

Be brave, she thought.

Just when she was sure that it wasn't going to happen, a figure stumbled from the forest.

His jeans were dirty, and briars had snagged in one of his shoelaces. Sweat darkened his shirt, and his hair looked rumpled.

Ryan Bell panted on the edge of the forest, then shouted behind him. There was an answering call, and a few moments later, Ana emerged from the forest. She was running a hand through her green hair when her gaze alighted on Fin.

"There." The word was audible, even across the river. Fin was aware of how much bigger the two adults were. How much faster. They could catch her, if they wanted.

But she was betting that one thing would matter more.

Fin dropped the cameras as if she'd been startled. It wasn't hard to look scared; fear clawed at her ribs, adrenaline making the world at once too fast and too slow. She turned and ran, leaving the cameras on the ground behind her. She tore up the logging road, toward the trees. She had to get to the forest and she'd be safe.

She heard the sound of churning gravel—then a grunt. Fin glanced over her shoulder and saw as Ryan launched himself over the chain-link barrier, running onto the bridge.

Perhaps it was Fin's imagination, but there was a slight rumble beneath her feet. Like something waking up.

From their perch, the ravens began to screech. Their eerie calls echoed through the woods, overlapping one another.

Fin didn't stop. She couldn't. She had to hope that the camera mattered more than an eleven-year-old girl. And finally she reached the forest.

Leaves slapped at Fin's face as she dashed into the trees. She spun around, skidding as she dove into the undergrowth. Chest heaving, she peered back through the bushes.

Ana Bell had rushed across the toll bridge too. She stopped at the cameras, kneeling beside them like a parent falling to the side of an injured child. Gently, she picked up one of the cameras and unclipped it from the holster, running her fingers over the plastic. Ryan had slowed; his chest rose and fell in ragged bellows, and he was favoring one leg over the other.

He was still heading for the forest.

Fin's pulse quickened. She pressed herself into the ground.

"Wait!" Ana's voice broke out, halting Ryan in place.

He glanced over his shoulder. "What?" Even that one word was breathless and hoarse.

"It's fine," said Ana, relief evident in every word. "The camera's fine. It's got all the pictures still on it. Those kids must not have known how to delete them."

Ryan stood, poised as if to keep striding toward the forest. His stance reminded Fin of a dog yearning to be let free of its leash, to chase and to hunt. His eyes flickered over the trees, his fingers clenched.

"Let's go," said Ana. She clipped the camera onto the holster and slung it around her shoulders. "We need to find Michael."

"But what about—" Ryan began to say.

"It's gone," said Ana. "I'm sorry, but it's gone. It's a wild animal in its natural habitat. Unless you've been hiding a tranq gun in your jacket or something, we're never going to catch it. Not now. Besides, we've got these. And we can always come back."

A long moment dragged out.

Fin held her breath.

Ryan's gaze roamed the forest, darting from shadow to shadow.

Finally he took a step back. Toward his sister. Toward town. "Okay," he said. "But now you've got to admit I was right. All those times you said I'd imagined seeing a monster. It wasn't a tree. I was right."

"Fine," said Ana. "You were right. And now this place is going to be our Nobel ticket."

Together they turned and walked across the bridge a second time. The cameras swung along Ana's sides and her green hair flashed in the afternoon light. Ryan cast one last look toward the forest. Toward Fin.

It was a silent promise.

The bushes behind Fin rustled. Before she could gasp, Cedar emerged from the undergrowth. Brie was in her arms, her whiskers drooping with exhaustion.

"Ana's got a point," whispered Cedar. "She still has the pictures."

"Yeah," said Fin quietly. "But it won't matter, now that she's crossed the bridge. Both of them did."

Cedar's eyes widened in realization.

Fin said, "I'll bet you anything what she and Ryan want most is proof of cryptids—which they got. But if what you said about the toll bridge is true, no one will believe them. That's what the toll bridge does, right? Grants your wish, but makes you wish you'd never wanted it in the first place?"

Understanding made Cedar smile. "You made them curse themselves. Oh, that's evil."

"I know," said Fin, a little regretfully. "I feel kind of bad."

"Don't." Cedar watched Ana and Ryan walk back toward town. "You think Ryan really did see a monster here when he was a kid?"

"No one believed him then," said Fin. She patted Brie. "Just like no one's going to believe him now."

TWENTY
The Forestkind

Fin and Cedar rode a shadow through the forest.

Penny carried them silently and without a single misstep. She found trails that only deer could see, tracing a path back toward the inn. Brie napped in Fin's arms, snoring squeakily.

They found Eddie and River in the woods behind the inn. They had been searching for the girls and the bigfoot, bickering between themselves. When Eddie saw Fin riding the shadow, he beamed up at her and said, "Okay, that's cool."

And then the four of them journeyed deeper into the forest. Into the old growth, keeping off the hiking trails and away from other people. Fin remembered the way to the rotted cabin, to the clearing of shield ferns and huge footprints.

"That way," said Fin, nudging the shadow on. Penny trotted forward, hooves finding purchase through the roots and the wildflowers and the steep slope downward. About a hundred feet ahead was a redwood cracked down the middle from an old storm wound. Fin slid from the shadow horse, Brie still in her arms. The bigfoot looked around with interest, and Fin set her on the ground. Cedar followed.

"Do you see anything?" asked Cedar, touching Penny's neck. The horse glanced from side to side and gave a small shake of her head.

"What are we looking for?" asked River.

"Her family," said Eddie. "Brie's, I mean. Not the shadow horse's. I don't know if shadows have family."

"I'm her family," said Cedar. "She's my shadow, after all."

"I don't see anything." Fin spun around in place. She even peered into the cracked bark of the lightning-struck tree, as if a bigfoot might be hiding inside. With a sigh, Fin stepped back.

"Maybe they moved on," said Eddie. "Maybe there's a different spot we'll have to take her."

"I hope not," said Fin. "It's almost dark and—"

Brie meeped.

It was a loud meep, echoing from the trees. Fin fell silent, and the others looked at the bigfoot. Brie had straightened to her full height, her tiny paws tucked up against her chest. Her nose was pointed to the air, whiskers twitching as she sniffed. She made that sound again—and Fin realized what she was doing.

Brie was calling for her family.

None of them spoke, waiting for an answer. But none came. Disappointment fell like a weight in Fin's stomach and she turned toward the others, to ask what they should do next.

Then the tree behind them *moved.*

Fin gasped, staggering back in surprise. It wasn't a tree, but it had blended in so well with the reddish bark that standing among the redwoods had rendered it nearly invisible. Fin gazed up at a creature with red-brown fur, mushrooms and moss growing around its neck like a ruff, and big dark eyes. It was at least fifteen feet tall, with narrow shoulders and a face that looked a little like an otter's.

The bigfoots hadn't arrived; they had been there all along. Silent and camouflaged.

That was how they stayed hidden, Fin thought. They blended into the trees so seamlessly that they looked to be part of the forest.

"Oh my goodness," whispered Cedar. River made a soft, scared sound and his shoulder knocked into Fin's. They all pressed together—Fin, River, Cedar, and Eddie.

Because *all* the trees began to move—bigfoots leaving their camouflage behind as they encircled the four kids. Penny pawed at the ground, her mane flowing like ink in water.

The bigfoots moved with a ponderous grace; they were giants in a giant forest. Their feet were huge, and their dark eyes warm and watchful.

Brie let out a chittering noise and darted out of Fin's grasp. She nuzzled the leg of one of the creatures, pressing her face into its fur. It leaned over, sniffing at Brie, then made a noise that sounded a bit like a cat's purr.

Another bigfoot stepped closer to the kids. River grasped at Fin's hand, as if he needed something to hold on to. She clung back, elated and terrified. Even if they were herbivores, the bigfoots were so large, it was like standing amid a herd of elephants. One of them could step on her and that would be it.

The closest bigfoot blew out a warm, unexpected breath.

River flinched, but he held his ground. Fin met the creature's eyes. Part of its fur had been singed along one arm and shoulder, and what looked like a healing burn shone in the late afternoon light.

"The burn," Fin whispered. "The *fires*. That's what's changing Aldermere."

"What?" said Cedar softly.

The bigfoot looked at them silently.

"Look at that one's arm," said Fin. She kept her voice soft, so as not to spook them. "I think—you remember what Mayor Downer said at the meeting? About the prescribed burn happening twenty miles away?"

Eddie inhaled sharply. "Oh. You think that's what separated Brie from her herd? That's what's driving the monsters closer to town? Fires?"

"What are we talking about?" said River in a small choked voice as the bigfoot's head swung toward him.

"They could have lost one another in the smoke or something," said Fin. "Fire disrupts magic. And scares animals."

The bigfoot regarded Fin and the others with its warm dark eyes. Then it straightened and made a soft noise—low and melodic as whale song. It must have been a command, because the others began to move. With heavy, ponderous strides, the bigfoot herd turned east toward the deepest part of the forest.

Brie looked back at Fin and the others. She meeped.

"*Meep,*" said Fin, her throat tight.

"Wait," said Eddie. He reached into his coat and withdrew something—a ragged-looking teddy bear. He tossed it into the air. Brie caught it and clung to the toy.

Brie meeped again. Then she scurried after her family.

The creatures vanished into the forest. The only trace of them was a faint tremor of the ground and a shiver of redwood needles overhead.

For a minute, no one dared to move. Then Eddie shifted on his feet, a twig snapping beneath his shoe. The sharp *crack* seemed to break the spell.

Fin drew in a breath.

"Whoa," said River. "That was—wow. I can't believe . . ." He was unable to put the experience into words. Like he had been witness to something rare and beautiful.

Fin knew how he felt.

They walked back to Aldermere.

Clouds gathered overhead, and the air smelled sharp and metallic. It looked as though it might rain—and Fin was glad for it. The rain would wash away any footprints, any last bit of evidence of Brie and her family.

Everyone was quiet, deep in their own thoughts. Fin was glad that no one was in the mood to talk; she was too exhausted to cobble together any semblance of normal conversation. By the time they reached the edges of town, a few drops of rain had begun to sprinkle from the sky.

As they walked by Mayor Downer's house, Fin saw the mayor herself pruning the flowers in her garden. "Hey, Mayor," said Eddie, waving.

Mayor Downer rose to her feet. She had protective pads on her knees, and her garden gloves looked well used. "Mr. Elloway. Ms. Barnes. Ms. Carver. And how do you prefer to be addressed?" The last question was directed at River, who jumped.

He looked around desperately, as if he hoped someone would answer for him. "I—uh. Mr. River is fine."

"Mr. River," said Mayor Downer. "I hope you're being made to feel welcome." It came out like more of a pronouncement than a question.

River swallowed. Fin saw him rub the scab along his knuckles. "I am. Uh. Ma'am," he added after a moment's awkward silence.

"Good," said Mayor Downer. She blew out a gusty breath. "Not an hour ago I saw one of the film crew run screaming down the street. It scared some of the other tourists. I wonder what could have disturbed him so."

"I think the internet went out at the inn again," said Fin earnestly.

Mayor Downer's gaze fell on her. "Perhaps that was it," she said, but not as if she believed it. "You stay out of trouble, now."

It was an obvious dismissal, so the four of them continued on. River didn't speak until they were well away. "That's the mayor?" he said quietly. "She's . . . terrifying."

"You get used to it," said Eddie. "If she tries to measure your lawn, just ignore her. And tell me. I'll sic my mom on her again."

River's brow scrunched in confusion, but he didn't ask. "Thanks."

They parted ways with smiles and weary waves—Cedar toward Brewed Awakening, River toward his house, and Eddie and Fin toward the cottage.

By the time they reached home, the rain had become a steady beat against Fin's coat. Dusk emerged from the shadows, spreading out along the ground. But the shadows looked more friendly than intimidating.

A familiar pair of headlights shone through the rain and the encroaching dark. A Ford Fiesta pulled into the driveway, and Aunt Myrtle got out. She wore her usual array of scarves and beaded jewelry, her long skirt rippling as she emerged from the car. "Hey," she called, seeing Fin and Eddie. "I decided to come back a little early."

"How was the art show?" asked Eddie. "Did you sell a lot of paintings?"

Aunt Myrtle reached out and gave Eddie a one-armed hug before looking him over. "I sold a few, but the show will be up for the next three weeks. I expect there'll be a few more buyers. Has everything been good here?"

Fin and Eddie glanced at each other.

"Your tents are in the woods behind the cottage," Fin blurted out. "Should we grab them before they get rained on?"

"Oh, you two camped in the woods?" said Aunt Myrtle. "Naw, they'll be fine for a night. We can dry them off in the morning." She put a hand on Fin's shoulder and one on Eddie's as they walked toward the big house. "Anything else exciting happen while I was gone?"

Fin looked out at the forest. "No, not really."

TWENTY-ONE
The Aftermath

The day SNACC broke the news that Bigfoot was real, Fin was trying to teach a raven to play fetch. Again.

She held a camera lens between her fingers. The glass gleamed in the sunlight. "Lens," said Fin. She tossed it into the soft overgrown grass of the big house's backyard. "Fetch."

Morri sat on a rusted wheelbarrow, grooming her feathers with lazy glee. So far she had fetched everything from River's glasses—which hadn't gone over well—to the forgotten quarter that Fin had lost in this very same lawn. She seemed to delight in retrieving anything that wasn't the lens. "You need to offer her a whole egg," said Eddie.

"She's going to get spoiled," said Fin.

"Can a raven get spoiled?" asked River. He sat on an old lawn chair, working on a book report. His notes kept rustling in the wind, and he'd weighed them down with a metal frog he'd found in Aunt Myrtle's garden.

"Don't feed the ravens for a week," said Eddie, his face utterly impassive, "and find out."

River frowned, like he knew Eddie was baiting him but didn't quite know how.

It was the last day of spring break, and all of them had gathered in the big house's backyard to finish up the last of their homework. Eddie was glumly planted in front of his math book, while Cedar put the finishing touches on a sketch for art class. She had spent several days working in Brewed Awakening to keep her parents from wondering why she had spent so much time at Fin's house.

For the rest of spring break, River had been coming over. He said it was because he needed to know more about the magic if he was going to live in Aldermere, but Fin suspected it had something to do with the fact that she'd forced Eddie to give up the big house's Wi-Fi password. And River was more tolerable these days. He wasn't rude, and he never forgot Cedar's name—which, Fin had to remind herself, hadn't been his fault. He couldn't have remembered Cedar until he believed in magic. And he had agreed not to mention anything about magic to his parents, under one condition.

"I'll keep this town's weird secrets. Just stop calling me River," he said. "I hate my last name. Scott sounds normal, at least."

"You know," said Cedar thoughtfully. "Scott River is an actual river in California."

"Yeah," said Scott sourly. "I know. My parents did that on purpose."

"Was that your parents' original last name or did they change it?" asked Cedar.

Scott scowled. "My parents were hippies living in Mendocino before they had me. What do you think?" His gaze flicked over her. "And you're one to talk, *Cedar Carver.*"

"Actually, my name was almost Cedar Espinoza," she said, grinning. "But when they got married, my dad took my mom's last name. She wrote books back then, so changing her name would've been confusing to her readers. Brand awareness and all."

"But they named you after a tree," said Scott.

"My dad likes trees," said Cedar. "I was almost Holly."

Scott threw a glance at Fin. "And what about you? Your mom into fishing or something?"

"Don't look at me," said Fin. "I'm named after our great-grandpa Finley."

"How is it," said Scott, as though every word pained him, "that Edward is the only one of us with a somewhat normal name?"

Eddie snorted. "Don't remind me. My name's so boring, it's embarrassing."

Mom came out of the cottage, holding a plate of sandwiches. She set them down on one of the lawn chairs, brushing away a bumblebee as it buzzed around the food. "Hey, kids," she said. "How's the last of the spring break homework? Did all of you save it for the last day?"

"I'm done," said Fin, a bit smugly. "Just trying to teach Morri to fetch again."

Mom cast a doubtful look at the raven on the wheelbarrow. "You . . . have fun with that."

Eddie groaned. "Math. I hate math. Why'd I put it off?"

Cedar picked up a sandwich. "I finished my art project, so now I'm here for the food."

"Well, I hope you like cheese and veggie, because there's not a lot else in the fridge," said Mom. "I need to go shopping soon. At least now I'll have the time, since our most demanding guests are gone." She let out a sigh.

"They left a rather rude review of the inn online, saying they couldn't ever get on the internet."

"Hopefully they won't come back," said Fin.

Mom nodded, gave Fin's shoulder a squeeze. It was then that Fin noticed Mom looked different. Her lipstick was a little darker and her fingernails were painted. Fin frowned at her. "Are you going to work?"

A faint flush suffused Mom's cheeks. She reached up and pushed a strand of hair behind her ear, as if she needed something to do with her hands. "Ah—no. I'm going to the diner."

Fin gaped at her. The diner had good food, but all the adults muttered about it being overpriced. Mom cooked or ate meals at the inn, where she was fed for free. Had something happened in the inn's kitchens? "Is Mr. Madeira's wife sick?" asked Fin. "Does he have to take care of her?" Guilt formed a familiar knot at the bottom of her stomach.

Mom shook her head. "Oh no. Nothing like that. I'm . . . meeting someone."

That was when it clicked. Mom had taken care with her makeup and was wearing a nice skirt. She was going on a *date*. Fin sputtered out a laugh, realized that probably wasn't the best response, and tried to keep a straight face. Mom didn't date. She'd always said she was too busy.

"Do I look that ridiculous?" asked Mom, smiling herself.

"No, you look great," answered Fin. "Who is it? If you say Mayor Downer, Aunt Myrtle might throw a fit."

"I'm sure she would," said Mom, laughing. "But no. I—I'm meeting Frank. If . . . I mean, are you okay with that?"

It shouldn't have come as a complete surprise. The potted rhododendrons were sitting beside the cottage's porch. But still there was a small voice in Fin that whispered that this was change, and change was bad and unknown and dangerous.

She tried her best to silence that voice. This was *Mom*. Who loved her and would always put her first, no matter what.

And Fin did like Frank. He was nice, fixed things, taught Eddie how to track through the woods, and he'd saved an abandoned ferret. She didn't think he would ever be cruel.

"I'm fine with it," said Fin.

"Good. I'll see you later." Mom dropped a kiss against Fin's hair and waved goodbye to the other kids before walking across the lawn and vanishing around the big house.

Fin waited until she was gone before looking at the others. "Has anyone checked the SNACC website today?"

They had made sure at least one of them looked at the website every day, to see if the new episode had gone up.

"I can." Scott dug his phone from his pocket.

"You think they're going to come back?" asked Cedar. Morri had fluttered to her shoulder, eyeing the sandwich in Cedar's hand. Cedar absentmindedly tore off a piece of crust and tossed it into the air. Morri grabbed it eagerly.

"I mean, Ryan said he wanted to," said Fin. "But after their encounter with the bridge, who knows? Maybe they're cursed, so that they'll never find the town again."

Scott sat up straighter. "Hey, it's up!"

"What?" Fin stepped away from the plate of sandwiches, her hunger replaced by nerves.

"Give me a second." Scott's finger darted across the touch screen of his phone with ease, but he frowned at the phone. "There's the episode and blog post . . . ah, yes. There are the pictures."

He scrolled down, and Fin held her breath. Cedar's fingers dug into her sandwich, leaving dents in the bread. Even Eddie was quiet.

"Okay," said Scott, holding up the phone. "It's . . . wow. It's kind of terrible."

Fin leaned in to look. Scott had blown the photo up so that it encompassed the whole phone screen.

There was a bright lens flare obscuring one corner of the picture—and as for the picture itself, Fin had to squint.

It was a little blurry, as if Michael's hands had been shaking when he took it. Brie stood there, with Fin kneeling beside her.

"It looks like they put swimming fins on a gopher," said Cedar.

"It does," said Eddie. "Everyone's going to think they dressed up an otter."

"None of the pictures show your face, Fin," said Scott. "They're all from the back. I can see your hair and your coat and that's pretty much it."

Some of Fin's fears unwound. She'd been worrying a little over her face being splashed across the internet in connection with Aldermere and Bigfoot—especially if her dad was still looking for her and Mom. She closed her eyes for a moment, then said, "What else did they say?"

"I can't tell much," said Scott. "I have to keep refreshing the page." He poked at his cell phone. "It keeps saying the server's offline."

"I told you," said Fin. "They're cursed by the toll bridge. Well, Ana and Ryan Bell are cursed. Michael is probably fine."

"He quit," said Scott, looking surprised. "I thought you saw. It went up on their social media feeds about two days after they left town. Said he wanted to pursue his dream career of filming nature documentaries in Australia."

"Oh no," said Cedar, looking both dismayed and amused. "I think I may have traumatized him."

"No shadow monsters in Australia," said Eddie. "Well, probably."

"It all worked out," said Cedar. "Brie's back with her family, SNACC only has a few pictures that no one will believe, and Aldermere is safe."

"Happy endings for all," said Eddie. "Except for the math homework." He plopped onto the ground, picking up his textbook with all the enthusiasm of Mom when she had to clean moldy food from the fridge.

Scott walked over to the tray of sandwiches, reaching for one. Fin followed him. Now that she was sure the footage wasn't going to blow up across the internet, her appetite had returned. Scott picked up one sandwich for himself and held out another to Fin. She took it with a nod of thanks. "I'm glad it worked out," said Scott. A flash of shame crossed his face. "I—I never really did apologize for what I did. I'm sorry, you know."

She took a bite of sandwich so she wouldn't have to answer right away. "Why'd you go to them?"

Scott sighed. "Because they looked like experts and that shadow thing was terrifying. You have to admit it.

Also . . . I mean, they were offering five hundred dollars for information. I thought, maybe we could go home if I got that money."

Fin winced a little. She understood the need for a home— it was why she'd worked so hard to protect Aldermere. "I get that." She took another bite. "You want to go home?"

"I mean, I still think this town is weird." Scott toyed with the edge of his sandwich. He pulled off a tiny bit of bread and tossed it into the air.

Morri caught it in midair, swooping by. Scott smiled at her.

"But there are upsides," he admitted. They stood in silence for a few moments, watching as Morri devoured the bread.

"So," said Fin. "I have to ask. How did the rivalry between you and Eddie start, anyways?"

"Eddie never told you?" asked Scott, surprised.

"He was always vague about it," said Fin. "And Cedar said something about a spider."

Scott blew out a breath. "It—it was in kindergarten."

"Seriously?" said Fin. "Did he steal your favorite markers or something?"

Scott laughed and rubbed at the back of his head. "No. He . . . uh. He brought his mom's tarot cards to school for show-and-tell. I told him magic wasn't real and fortune-tellers were frauds."

Fin shook her head, smiling despite herself. "Of course you did."

"Well, as far as I knew, it was true." Scott held out an arm, gesturing all around them. "How could I know magic was real? It's not supposed to be. Which reminds me—if Bigfoot is real, what else is? The Loch Ness monster? Witches? That squirroose thing Edward was talking about?"

Morri alighted on Fin's shoulder. Fin reached up, ruffling the soft feathers around the raven's neck. Fin glanced toward Cedar; her shadow was gone. Which meant somewhere out in the woods, an inky mare would be galloping through the forest. In that same forest, a baby bigfoot would be with her family. And as for what else lived out there . . .

Fin reached into her coat pocket, her fingers tangling around the chain of the old locket. "Maybe we'll find out."

Acknowledgments

Hello, dear reader. Thank you for joining me on this little journey back to Aldermere. While I love every book I've written, this series is particularly dear to me. So thank you for your support. Whether you purchased this book in a bookstore, listened to the audio, checked it out from a library, or borrowed it from a friend, I truly appreciate your taking the time to read it. The best magic I've found is in the pages of books, and that magic needs readers to flourish.

To my agent, Sarah Landis, who is my fiercest advocate and a joy to work with, thank you for your constant support, your fabulous edits, and the phone calls, which always leave me smiling. To everyone at Sterling Lord Literistic, I appreciate you so much. And to Berni Barta, thanks for your unwavering encouragement and hard work.

I am humbled and privileged to work with a wonderful team at Greenwillow. I owe so much to my insightful and skilled editor, Martha Mihalick. Thank you for helping me shape Aldermere into the world I hoped it could become. Thank you to Izzy Burton for illustrating such a gorgeous cover and to Sylvie Le Floc'h for making this entire book so beautiful. The biggest of thanks to Virginia Duncan, Lois Adams, Arianna Robinson, Vaishali Nayak, and Delaney Heisterkamp. And of course, to everyone at Shelf Stuff! Sending hugs to all of you.

To the lovely authors who read *Unseen Magic*, the first book in this series, in its early days—Margaret Peterson Haddix, Heather Kassner, and Jenn Reese—thank you for your kind words. And thanks to all the authors who have encouraged me as I waded into the middle grade genre.

To the booksellers, librarians, and teachers who continue to spread the joy of reading, thank you so much. And specifically, thanks to some of Aldermere's earliest visitors: Kalie Barnes-Young, Kel Russell, Lillian Tschudi-Campbell, Gabrielle Belisle, Alysha Welliver, and Alex Abraham.

To my family and friends. For everything. Thank you.